HOTEL TRANSYLVANIA

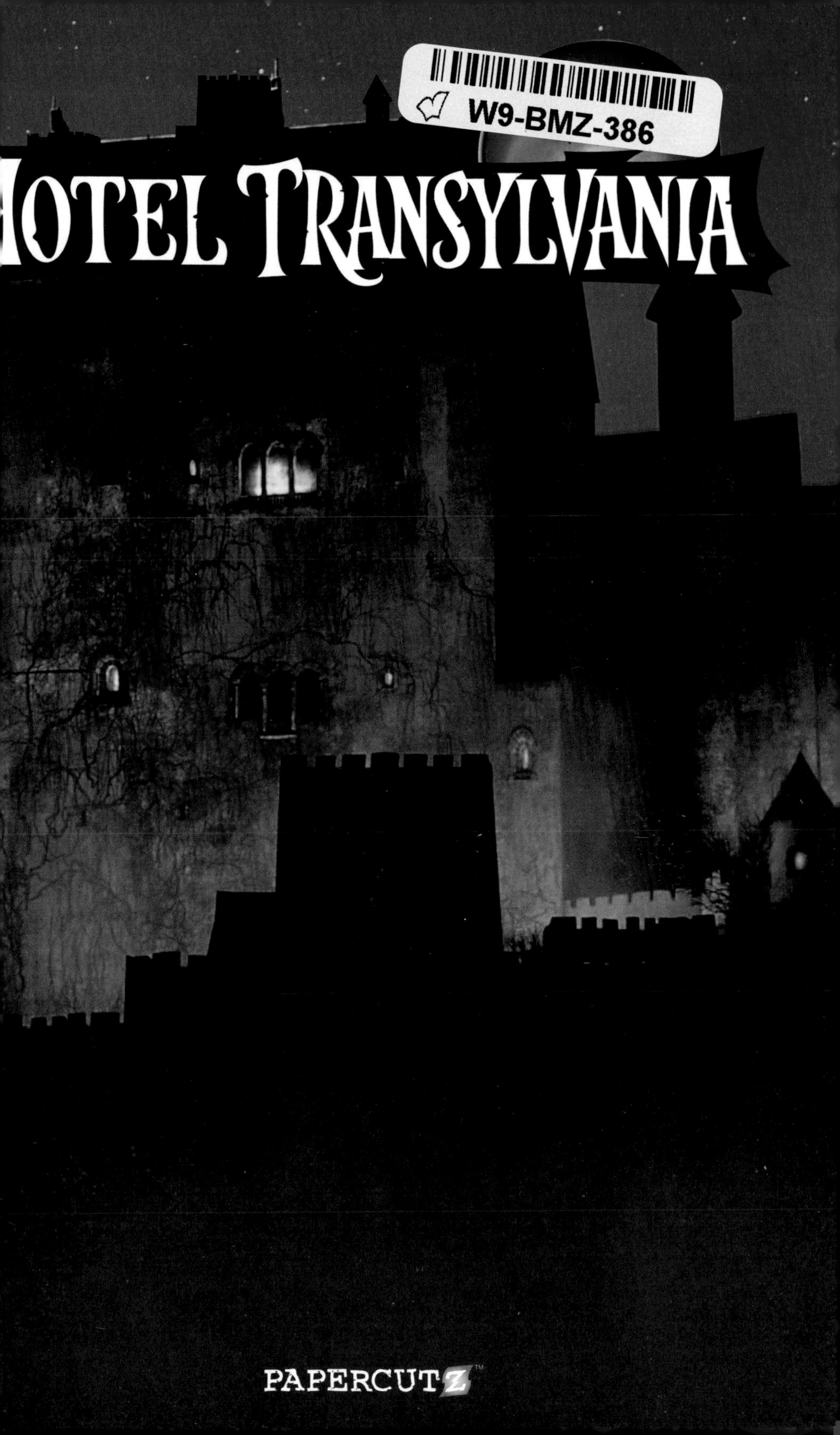

PAPERCUTZ™

MORE GREAT GRAPHIC NOVEL SERIES AVAILABLE FROM PAPERCUT

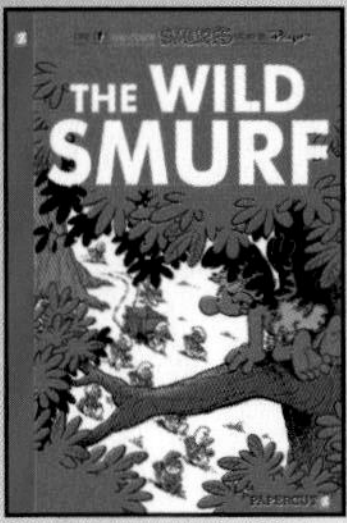
THE WILD SMURF
PAPERCUTZ
THE SMURFS #21

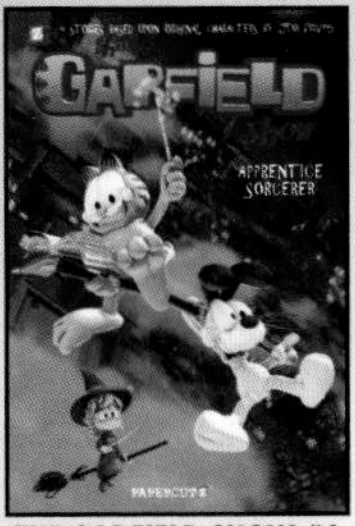
GARFIELD
APPRENTICE SORCERER
PAPERCUTZ
THE GARFIELD SHOW #6

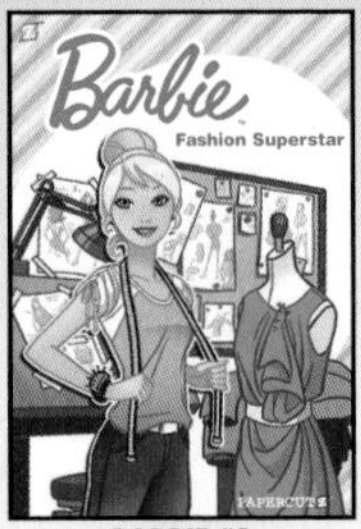
Barbie
Fashion Superstar
PAPERCUTZ
BARBIE #1

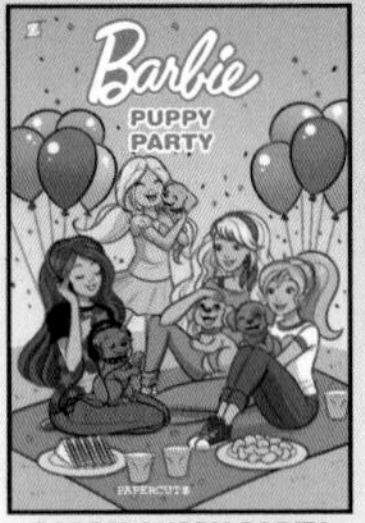
Barbie
PUPPY PARTY
PAPERCUTZ
BARBIE PUPPY PARTY

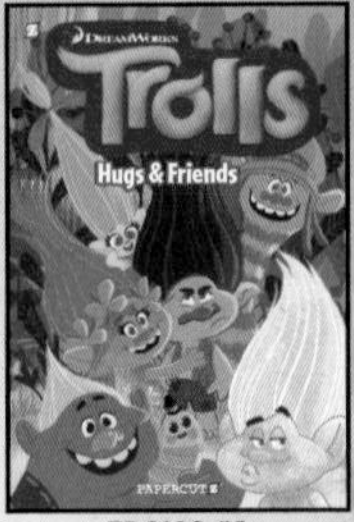
DreamWorks
Trolls
Hugs & Friends
PAPERCUTZ
TROLLS #1

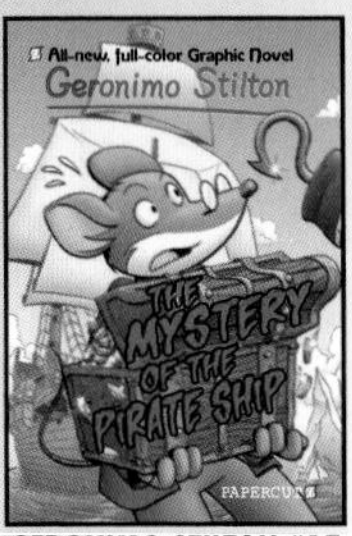
All-new, full-color Graphic Novel
Geronimo Stilton
THE MYSTERY OF THE PIRATE SHIP
PAPERCUTZ
GERONIMO STILTON #17

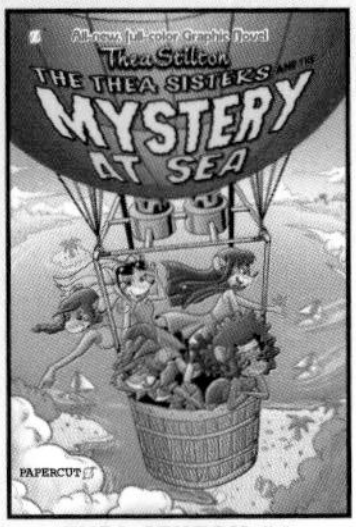
All-new, full-color Graphic Novel
Thea Stilton
THE THEA SISTERS
MYSTERY AT SEA
PAPERCUTZ
THEA STILTON #6

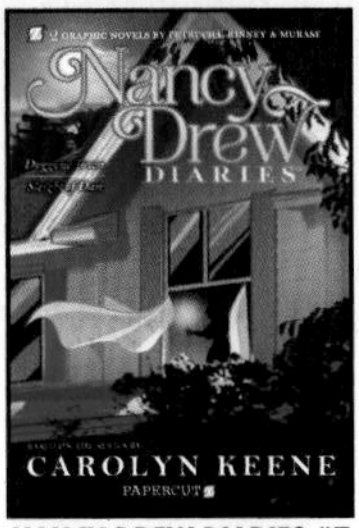
Nancy Drew
DIARIES
CAROLYN KEENE
PAPERCUTZ
NANCY DREW DIARIES #7

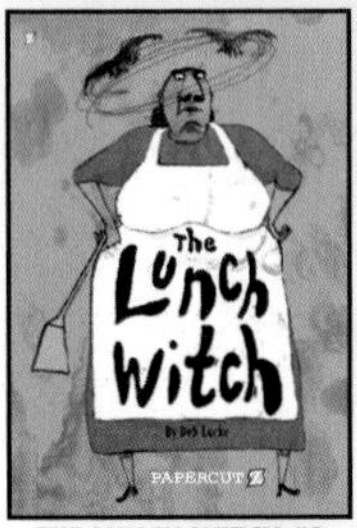
The Lunch Witch
PAPERCUTZ
THE LUNCH WITCH #1

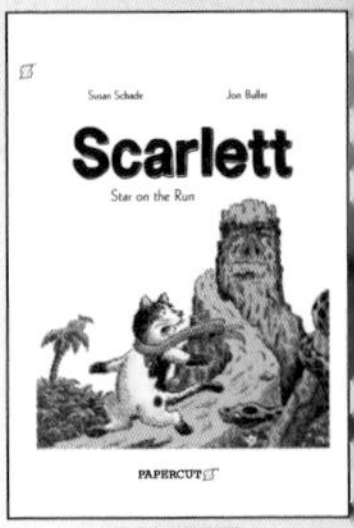
Susan Schade
Jon Buller
Scarlett
Star on the Run
PAPERCUTZ
SCARLETT

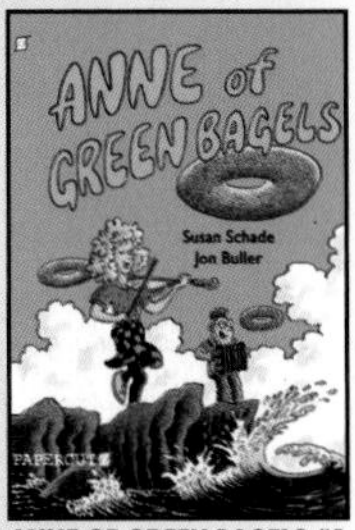
ANNE of GREEN BAGELS
Susan Schade
Jon Buller
PAPERCUTZ
ANNE OF GREEN BAGELS #1

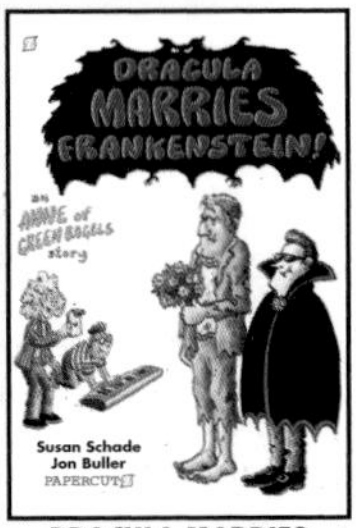
DRACULA MARRIES FRANKENSTEIN!
an ANNE of GREEN BAGELS story
Susan Schade
Jon Buller
PAPERCUTZ
DRACULA MARRIES FRANKENSTEIN!

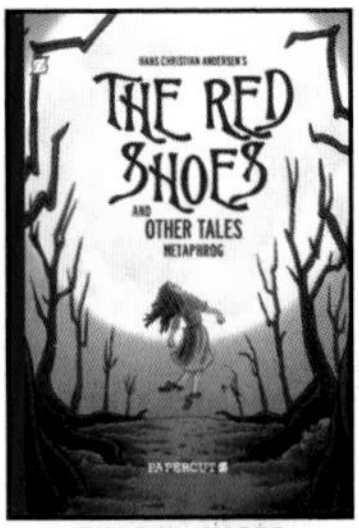
HANS CHRISTIAN ANDERSEN'S
THE RED SHOES
AND OTHER TALES
METAPHROG
PAPERCUTZ
THE RED SHOES

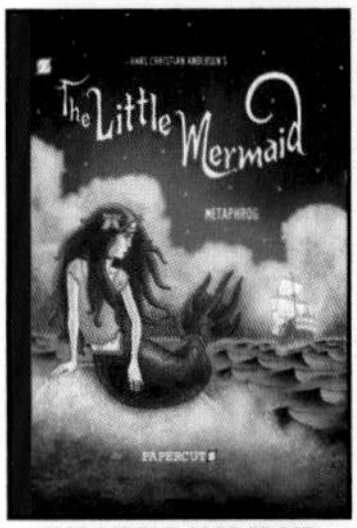
HANS CHRISTIAN ANDERSEN'S
The Little Mermaid
METAPHROG
PAPERCUTZ
THE LITTLE MERMAID

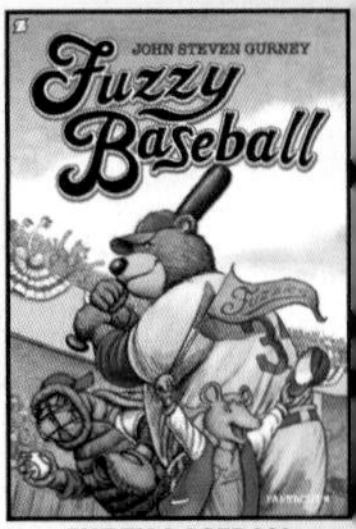
JOHN STEVEN GURNEY
Fuzzy Baseball
FUZZY BASEBALL

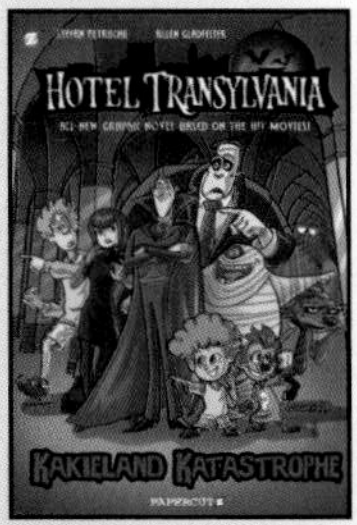
HOTEL TRANSYLVANIA
KAKIELAND KATASTROPHE
PAPERCUTZ
HOTEL TRANSYLVANIA #1

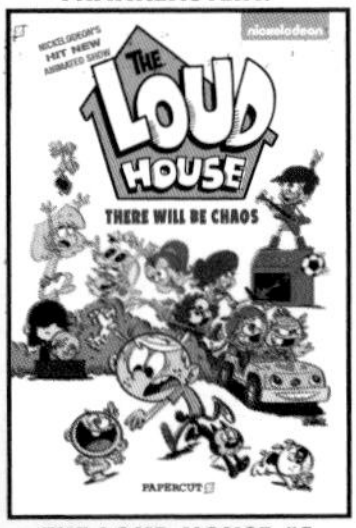
nickelodeon
THE LOUD HOUSE
THERE WILL BE CHAOS
PAPERCUTZ
THE LOUD HOUSE #1

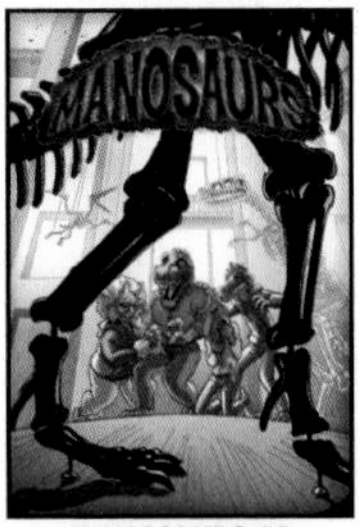
MANOSAURS
MANOSAURS #1

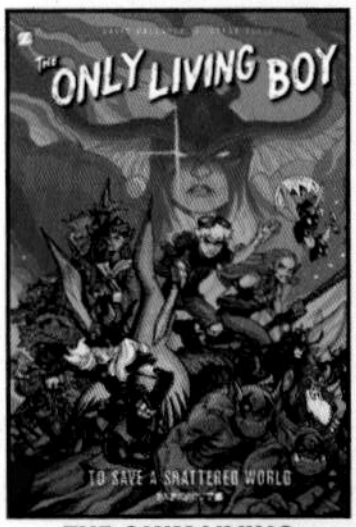
THE ONLY LIVING BOY
TO SAVE A SHATTERED WORLD
THE ONLY LIVING BOY #5

THE SMURFS, THE GARFIELD SHOW, BARBIE, HOTEL TRANSYLVANIA, MANOSAURS, THE LOUD HOUSE and TROLLS graphic novel available for $7.99 in paperback, and $12.99 in hardcover. THE ONLY LIVING BOY graphic novels are available for $8.99 in paperbo $13.99 in hardcover. GERONIMO STILTON and THEA STILTON graphic novels are available for $9.99 in hardcover only. FUZZY BASI graphic novels are available for $9.99 in paperback only. THE LUNCH WITCH, SCARLETT, and ANNE OF GREEN BAGELS graphic nov available for $14.99 in paperback only. THE RED SHOES and THE LITTLE MERMAID graphic novels are available for $12.99 in hardcov DRACULA MARRIES FRANKENSTEIN graphic novels are available for $12.99 in paperback only.

Available from booksellers everywhere. You can also order online from www.papercutz.com. Or call 1-800-886-1223, Monday through 9–5 EST. MC, Visa, and AmEx accepted. To order by mail, please add $5.00 for postage and handling for first book ordered, $1.00 fo additional book and make check payable to NBM Publishing. Send to: Papercutz, 160 Broadway, Suite 700, East Wing, New York, NY

THE SMURFS, THE GARFIELD SHOW, THE LOUD HOUSE, THE ONLY LIVING BOY, BARBIE, TROLLS, GERONIMO STILTON, THEA STIL FUZZY BASEBALL, THE LUNCH WITCH, THE LITTLE MERMAID, HOTEL TRANSYLVANIA, MANOSAURS, THE RED SHOES, ANNE OF C BAGELS, and SCARLETT graphic novels are also available wherever e-books are sold.

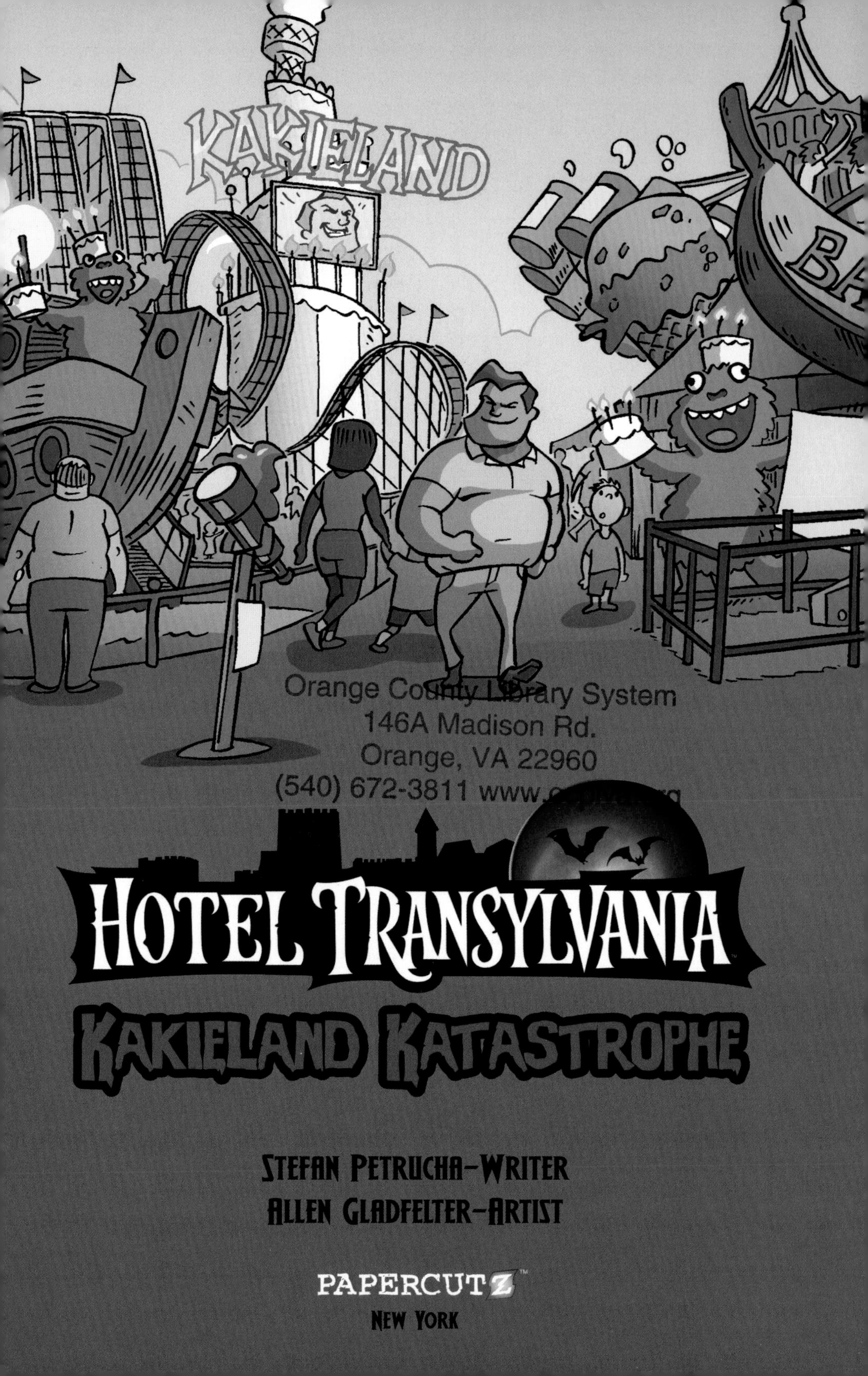
KAKIELAND

HOTEL TRANSYLVANIA™

KAKIELAND KATASTROPHE

STEFAN PETRUCHA–WRITER
ALLEN GLADFELTER–ARTIST

PAPERCUTZ™
NEW YORK

#1 Kakieland Katastrophe
Stefan Petrucha—Writer
Allen Gladfelter—Artist
Laurie E. Smith—Colorist [pages 1-30]
Matt Herms—Colorist [pages 31-50]
Wilson Ramos Jr.—Letterer
Production—Dawn Guzzo
Assistant Managing Editor—Jeff Whitman
Jim Salicrup
Editor-in-Chief

Special Thanks to James Silvani, Keith Baxter, Melissa Sturm,
Virginia King and everyone at Sony Pictures Animation

ISBN: 978-1-62991-808-2 paperback edition
ISBN: 978-1-62991-809-9 hardcover edition

Sony Pictures Animation

Papercutz books may be purchased for business or promotional
use. For information on bulk purchases please contact Macmillan
Corporate and Premium Sales Department at
(800) 221-795 x5442.

Printed in USA
September 2017

Distributed by Macmillan
First Printing

HOTEL TRANSYLVANIA

DRAC

Legendary monster, hotelier
extraordinaire and loving father,
Drac is finally enjoying the perks
of a monster AND human filled
Hotel Transylvania. Running
your own business can be a
pain in the neck but running a
family business along with being
the most legendary monster in
history is biting off a little more
than he can chew! But luckily
he's got the trusty Drac Pack by
his side and his loyal and ever-
loving daughter, Mavis.

HOTEL TRANSYLVANIA™

MAVIS

Juggling work at Hotel Transylvania and being an awesome mother, wife and daughter, Mavis does it all! She's curious, optimistic and deeply loyal to her monster and human family. While she relishes being her own vampire, she will always be daddy's little bat.

HOTEL TRANSYLVANIA™

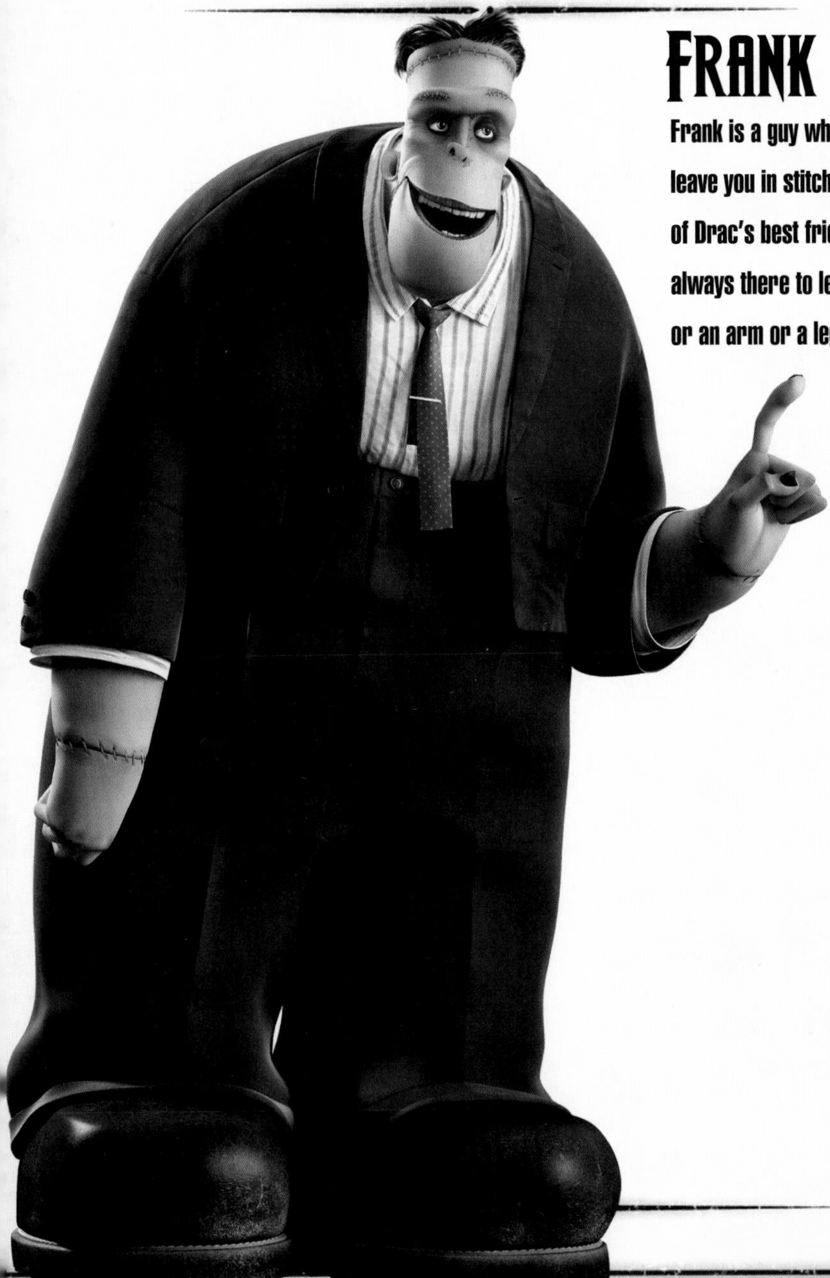

FRANK

Frank is a guy who will always leave you in stitches! He's one of Drac's best friends and is always there to lend a hand, or an arm or a leg.

HOTEL TRANSYLVANIA

MURRAY

Murray is literally the firmly wrapped fixture of the Drac Pack...because he's a mummy! He is the life of the party and is always there in a pinch to bandage any problem Drac may have.

HOTEL TRANSYLVANIA

DENNIS

All vampires have until their fifth
birthday to sprout their fangs...
and wouldn't you know it...
Mavis and Johnny's son did!
Dennis is a curly-haired, curious
kid, who just wants to sneak off
and have adventures with his
best wolf pup friend, Winnie.

HOTEL TRANSYLVANIA

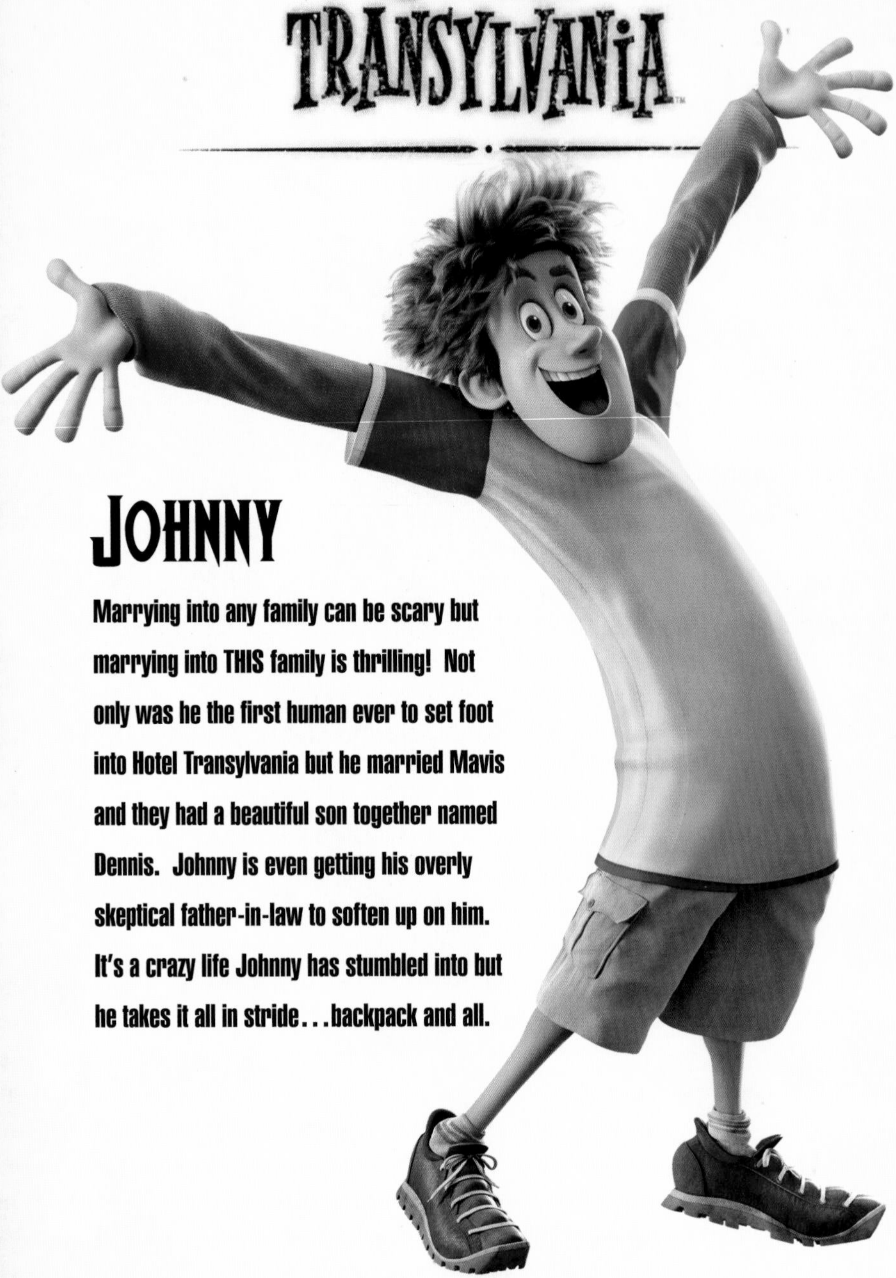

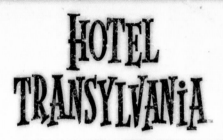

JOHNNY

Marrying into any family can be scary but marrying into THIS family is thrilling! Not only was he the first human ever to set foot into Hotel Transylvania but he married Mavis and they had a beautiful son together named Dennis. Johnny is even getting his overly skeptical father-in-law to soften up on him. It's a crazy life Johnny has stumbled into but he takes it all in stride. . .backpack and all.

HOTEL TRANSYLVANIA™

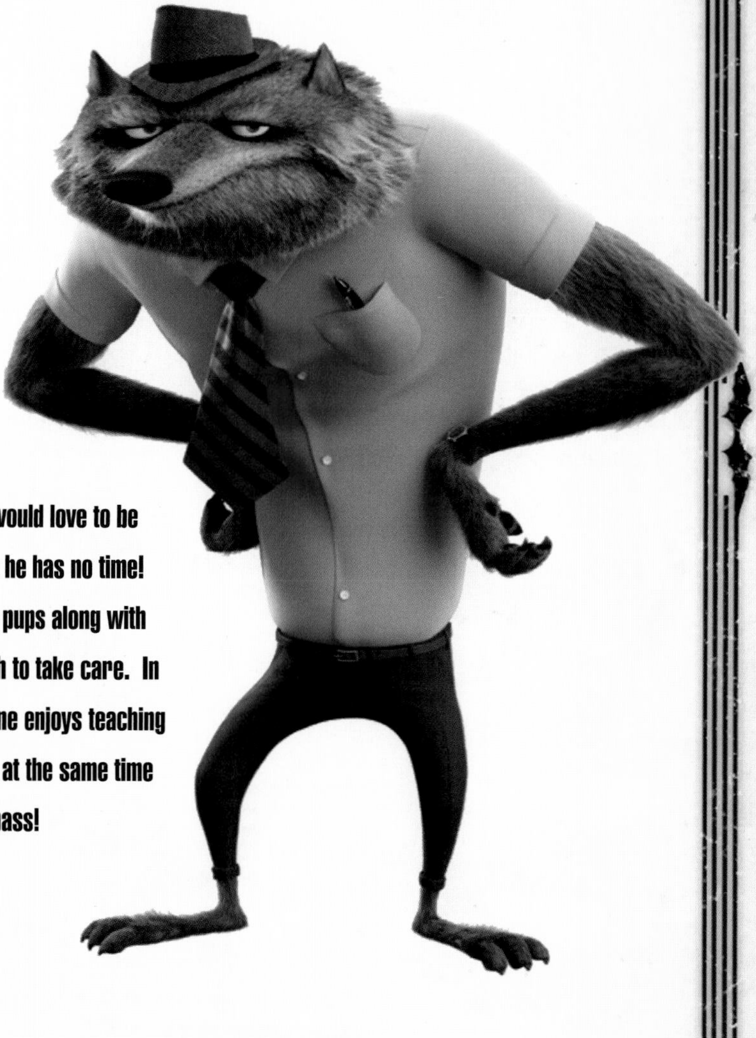

WAYNE

Wayne, the werewolf, would love to be howling at the moon but he has no time! He's got a gazillion wolf pups along with his wife Wanda of which to take care. In his little free time, Wayne enjoys teaching tennis and playing fetch at the same time as well as rocking the bass!

HOTEL TRANSYLVANIA

WINNIE

She's one of Wayne and Wanda's numerous pups. She's wild, rambunctious and always game for a mischievous adventure. She also has a not-so-secret crush on Dennis.

HOTEL TRANSYLVANIA

BLOBBY

This blob monster is always wiggling and jiggling for a good time! Semi-transparent and unassuming, Blobby is the one friend that everyone counts on in the group. He's even his own lost and found— you never know what you'll find in his goo!

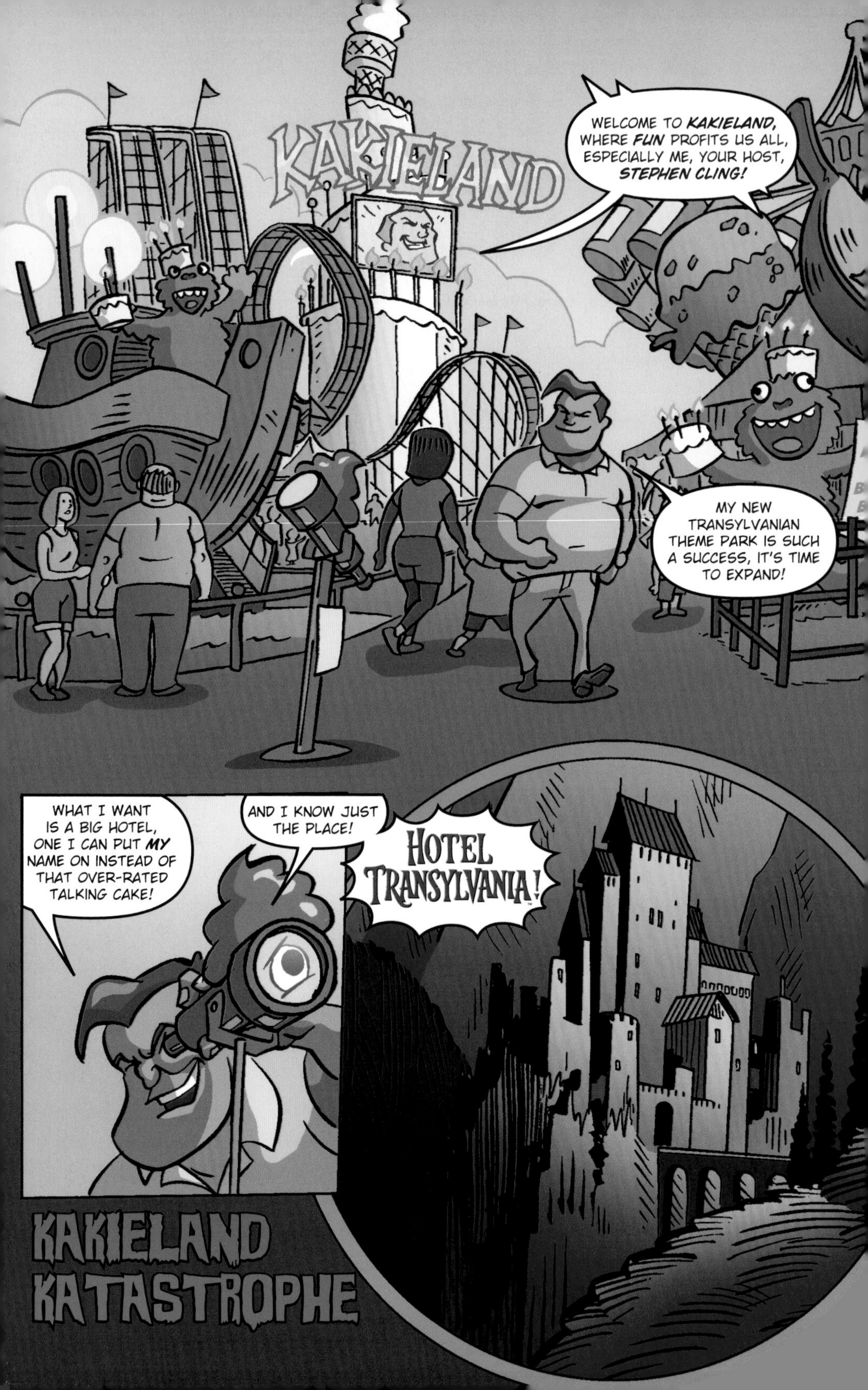
KAKIELAND
WELCOME TO KAKIELAND, WHERE FUN PROFITS US ALL, ESPECIALLY ME, YOUR HOST, STEPHEN CLING!
MY NEW TRANSYLVANIAN THEME PARK IS SUCH A SUCCESS, IT'S TIME TO EXPAND!
WHAT I WANT IS A BIG HOTEL, ONE I CAN PUT MY NAME ON INSTEAD OF THAT OVER-RATED TALKING CAKE!
AND I KNOW JUST THE PLACE!
HOTEL TRANSYLVANIA!
KAKIELAND KATASTROPHE

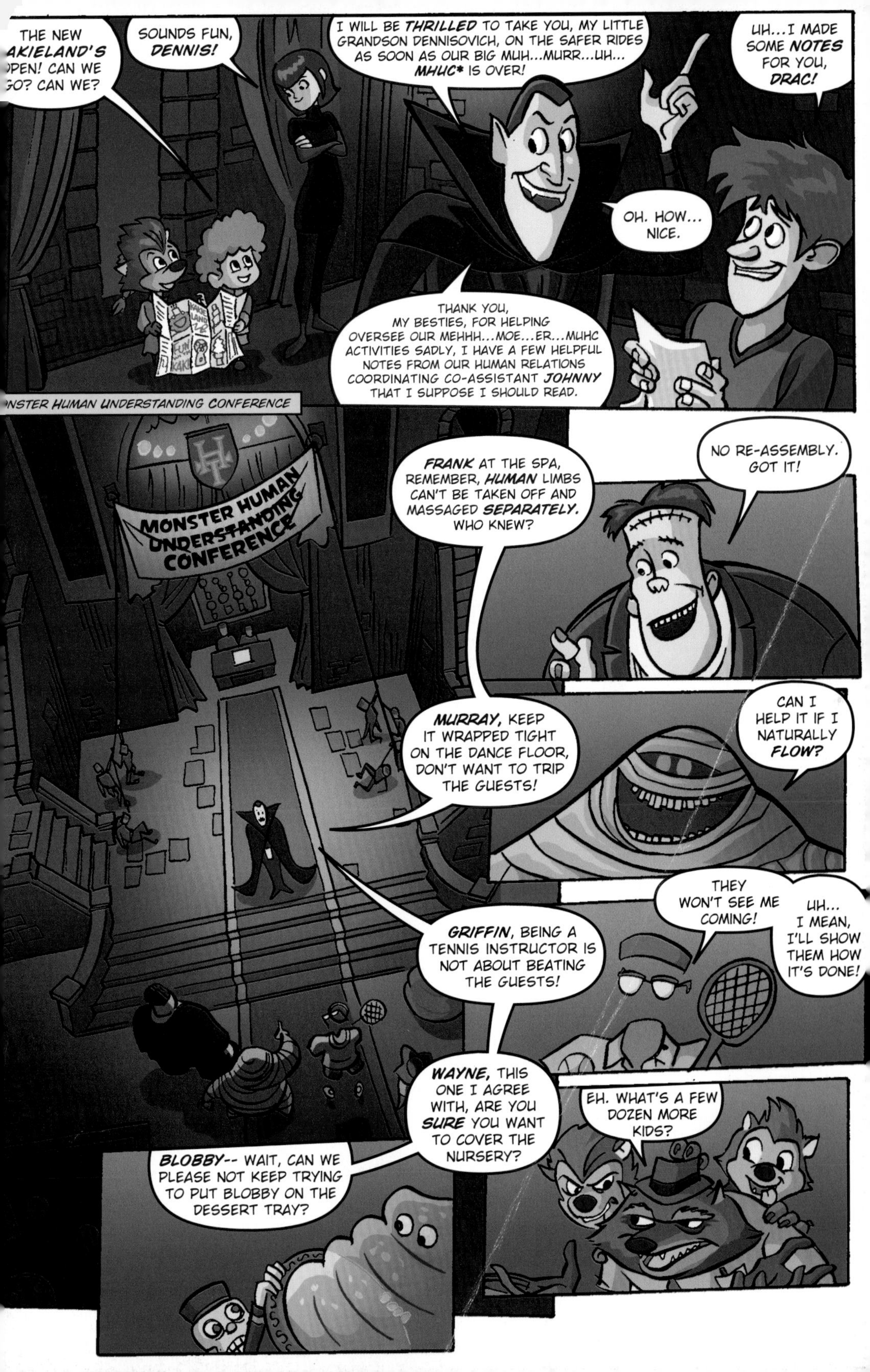
THE NEW AKIELAND'S OPEN! CAN WE GO? CAN WE?
SOUNDS FUN, DENNIS!
I WILL BE THRILLED TO TAKE YOU, MY LITTLE GRANDSON DENNISOVICH, ON THE SAFER RIDES AS SOON AS OUR BIG MUH...MURR...UH... MHUC* IS OVER!
UH...I MADE SOME NOTES FOR YOU, DRAC!
OH. HOW... NICE.
THANK YOU, MY BESTIES, FOR HELPING OVERSEE OUR MEHHH...MOE...ER...MUHC ACTIVITIES SADLY, I HAVE A FEW HELPFUL NOTES FROM OUR HUMAN RELATIONS COORDINATING CO-ASSISTANT JOHNNY THAT I SUPPOSE I SHOULD READ.
NSTER HUMAN UNDERSTANDING CONFERENCE
MONSTER HUMAN UNDERSTANDING CONFERENCE
FRANK AT THE SPA, REMEMBER, HUMAN LIMBS CAN'T BE TAKEN OFF AND MASSAGED SEPARATELY. WHO KNEW?
NO RE-ASSEMBLY. GOT IT!
MURRAY, KEEP IT WRAPPED TIGHT ON THE DANCE FLOOR, DON'T WANT TO TRIP THE GUESTS!
CAN I HELP IT IF I NATURALLY FLOW?
GRIFFIN, BEING A TENNIS INSTRUCTOR IS NOT ABOUT BEATING THE GUESTS!
THEY WON'T SEE ME COMING!
UH... I MEAN, I'LL SHOW THEM HOW IT'S DONE!
WAYNE, THIS ONE I AGREE WITH, ARE YOU SURE YOU WANT TO COVER THE NURSERY?
EH. WHAT'S A FEW DOZEN MORE KIDS?
BLOBBY-- WAIT, CAN WE PLEASE NOT KEEP TRYING TO PUT BLOBBY ON THE DESSERT TRAY?

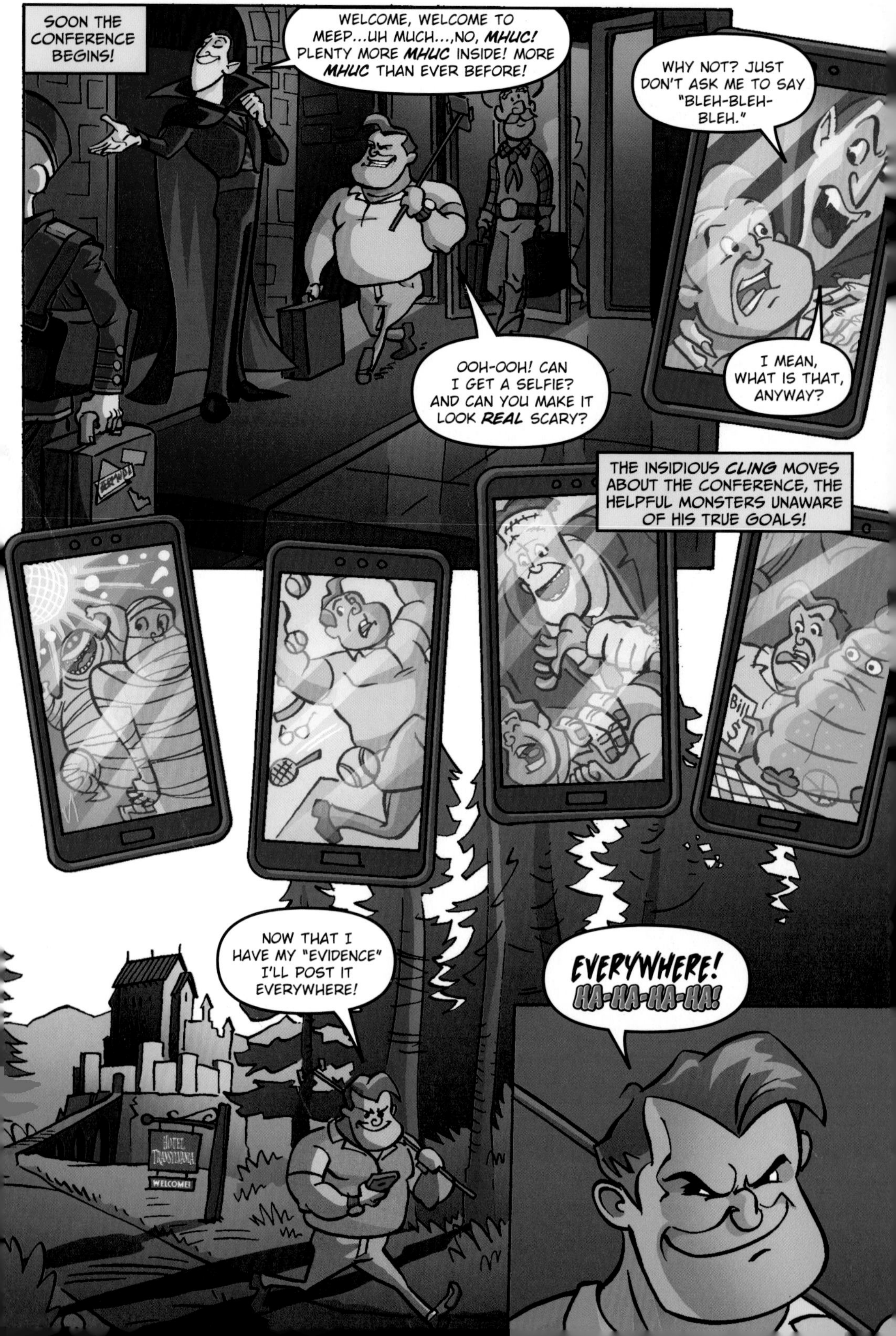
SOON THE CONFERENCE BEGINS!
WELCOME, WELCOME TO MEEP...UH MUCH...,NO, MHUC! PLENTY MORE MHUC INSIDE! MORE MHUC THAN EVER BEFORE!
OOH-OOH! CAN I GET A SELFIE? AND CAN YOU MAKE IT LOOK REAL SCARY?
WHY NOT? JUST DON'T ASK ME TO SAY "BLEH-BLEH-BLEH."
I MEAN, WHAT IS THAT, ANYWAY?
THE INSIDIOUS CLING MOVES ABOUT THE CONFERENCE, THE HELPFUL MONSTERS UNAWARE OF HIS TRUE GOALS!
Bill $
HOTEL TRANSYLVANIA
WELCOME!
NOW THAT I HAVE MY "EVIDENCE" I'LL POST IT EVERYWHERE!
EVERYWHERE!
HA-HA-HA-HA!

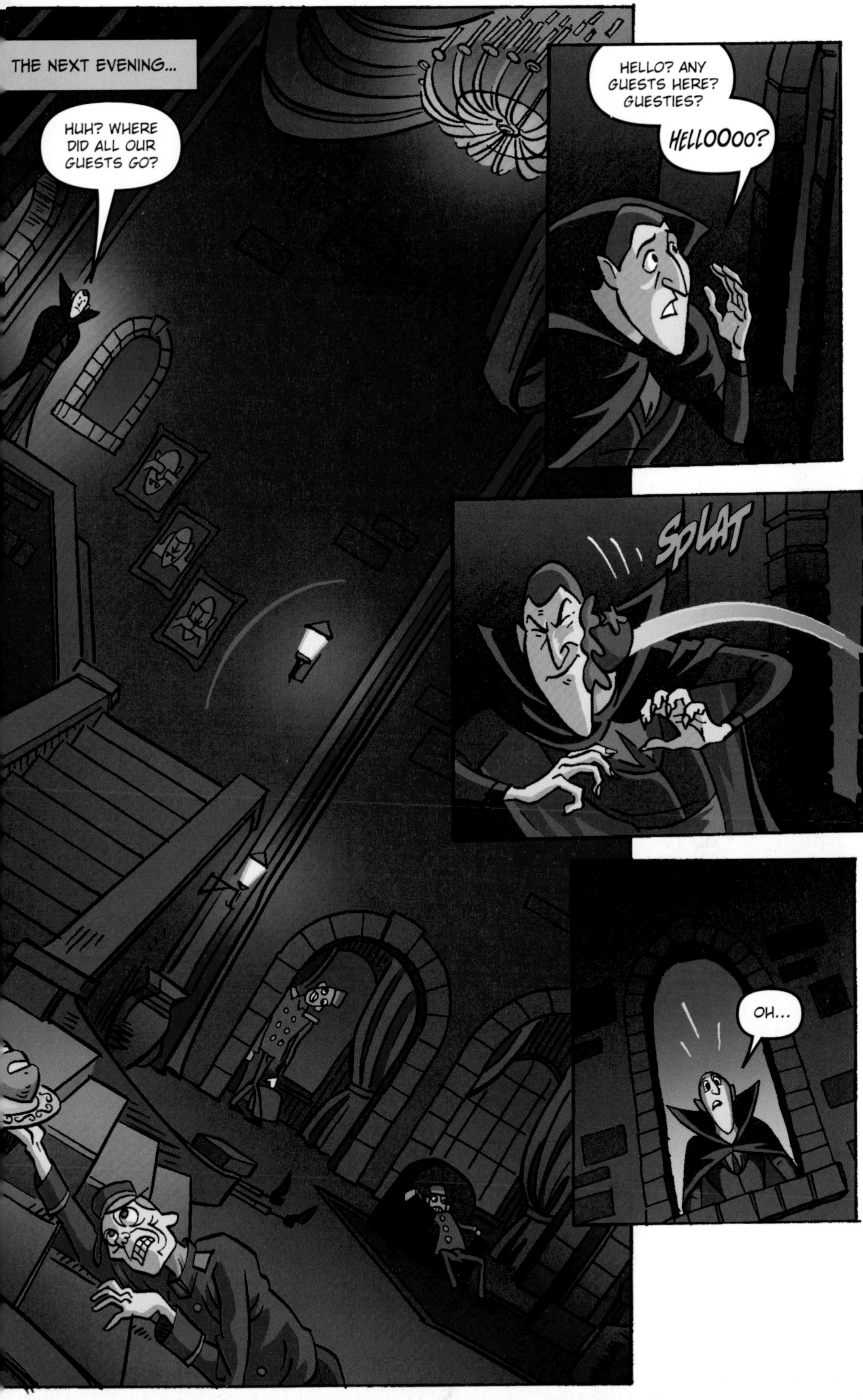
THE NEXT EVENING...
HUH? WHERE DID ALL OUR GUESTS GO?
HELLO? ANY GUESTS HERE? GUESTIES?
HELLOOOO?
SPLAT
OH...

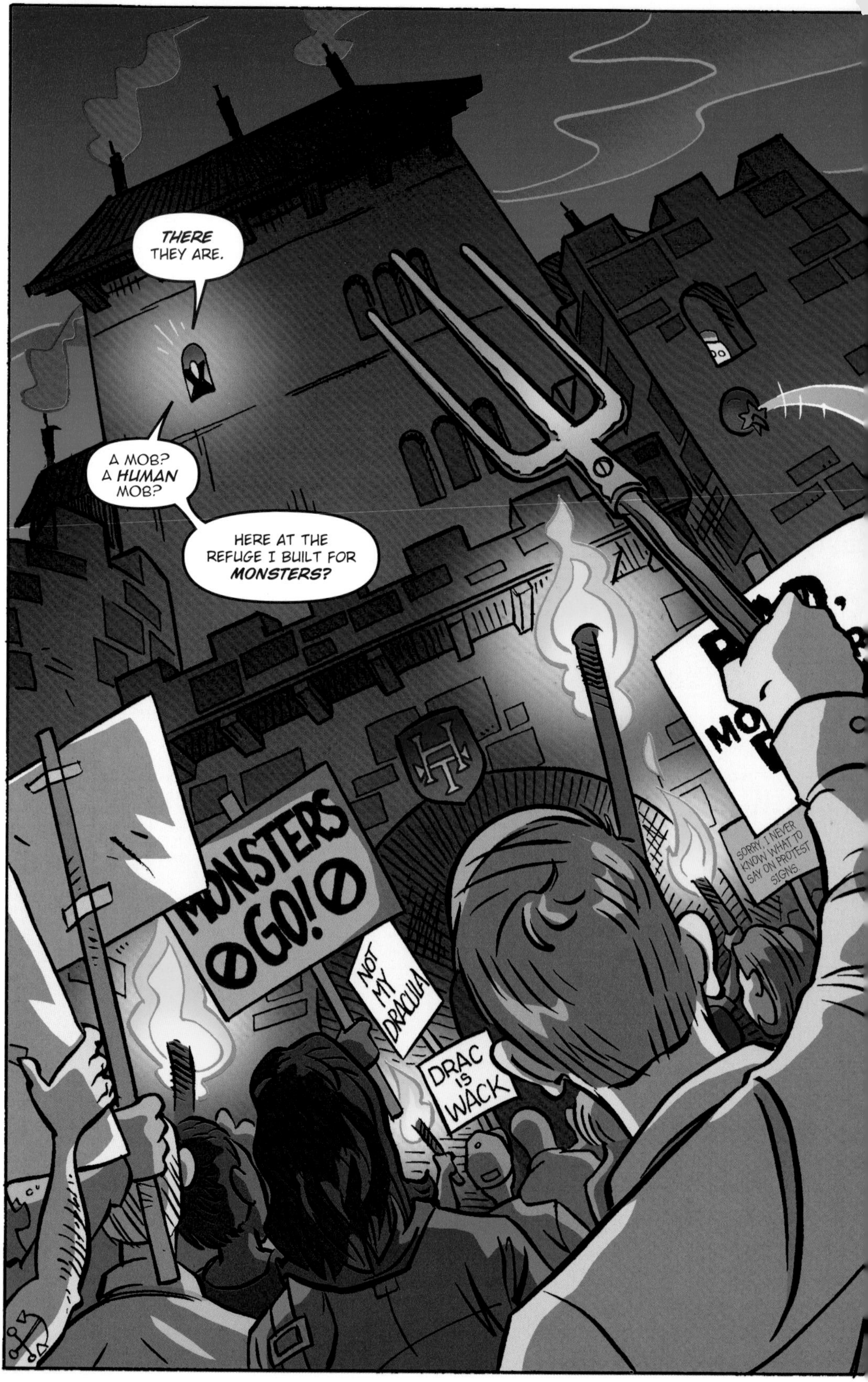

THERE THEY ARE.
A MOB? A HUMAN MOB?
HERE AT THE REFUGE I BUILT FOR MONSTERS?
MONSTERS GO!
NOT MY DRACULA
DRAC IS WACK
SORRY, I NEVER KNOW WHAT TO SAY ON PROTEST SIGNS.

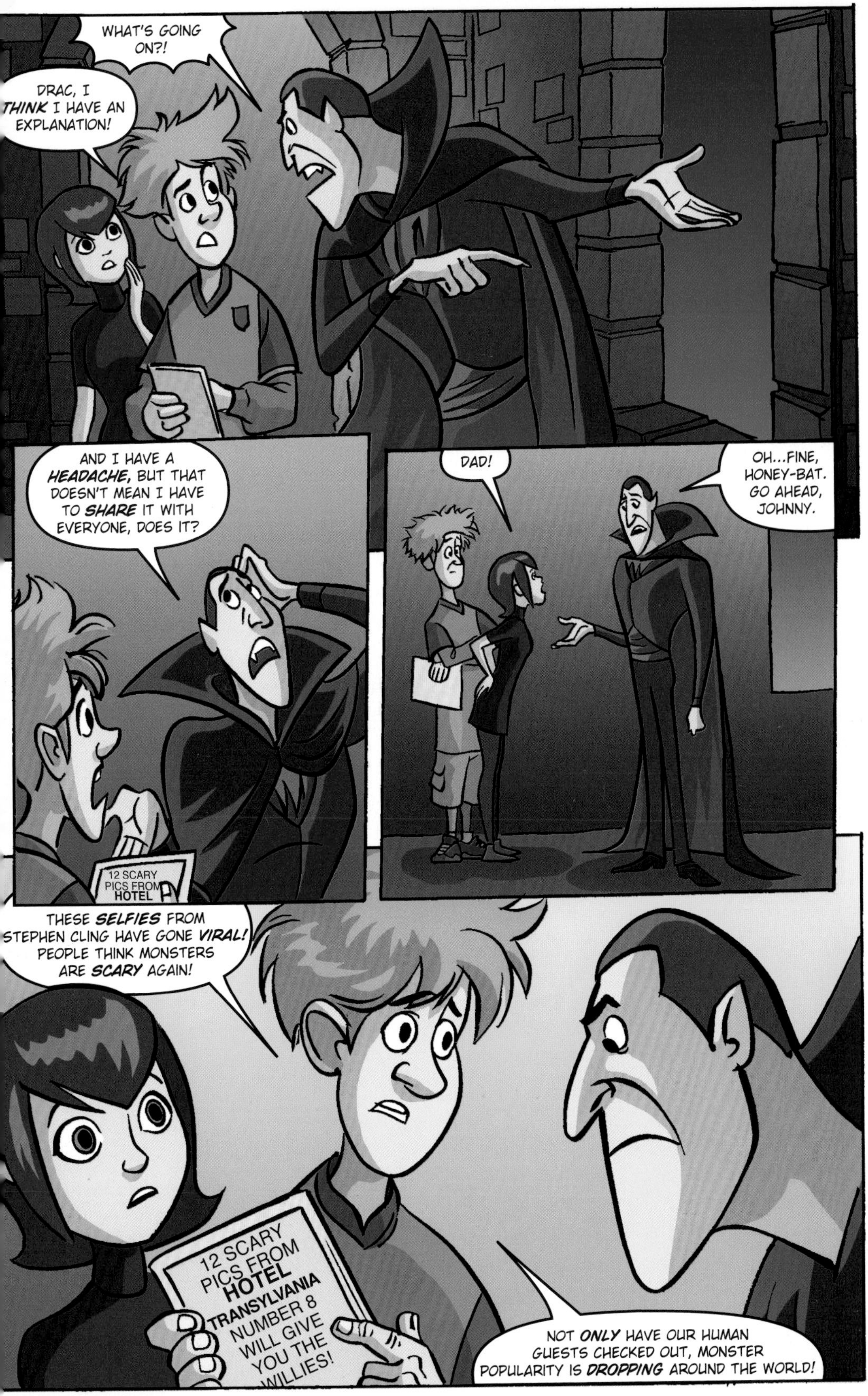
WHAT'S GOING ON?!
DRAC, I THINK I HAVE AN EXPLANATION!
AND I HAVE A HEADACHE, BUT THAT DOESN'T MEAN I HAVE TO SHARE IT WITH EVERYONE, DOES IT?
12 SCARY PICS FROM HOTEL
DAD!
OH...FINE, HONEY-BAT. GO AHEAD, JOHNNY.
THESE SELFIES FROM STEPHEN CLING HAVE GONE VIRAL! PEOPLE THINK MONSTERS ARE SCARY AGAIN!
12 SCARY PICS FROM HOTEL TRANSYLVANIA NUMBER 8 WILL GIVE YOU THE WILLIES!
NOT ONLY HAVE OUR HUMAN GUESTS CHECKED OUT, MONSTER POPULARITY IS DROPPING AROUND THE WORLD!

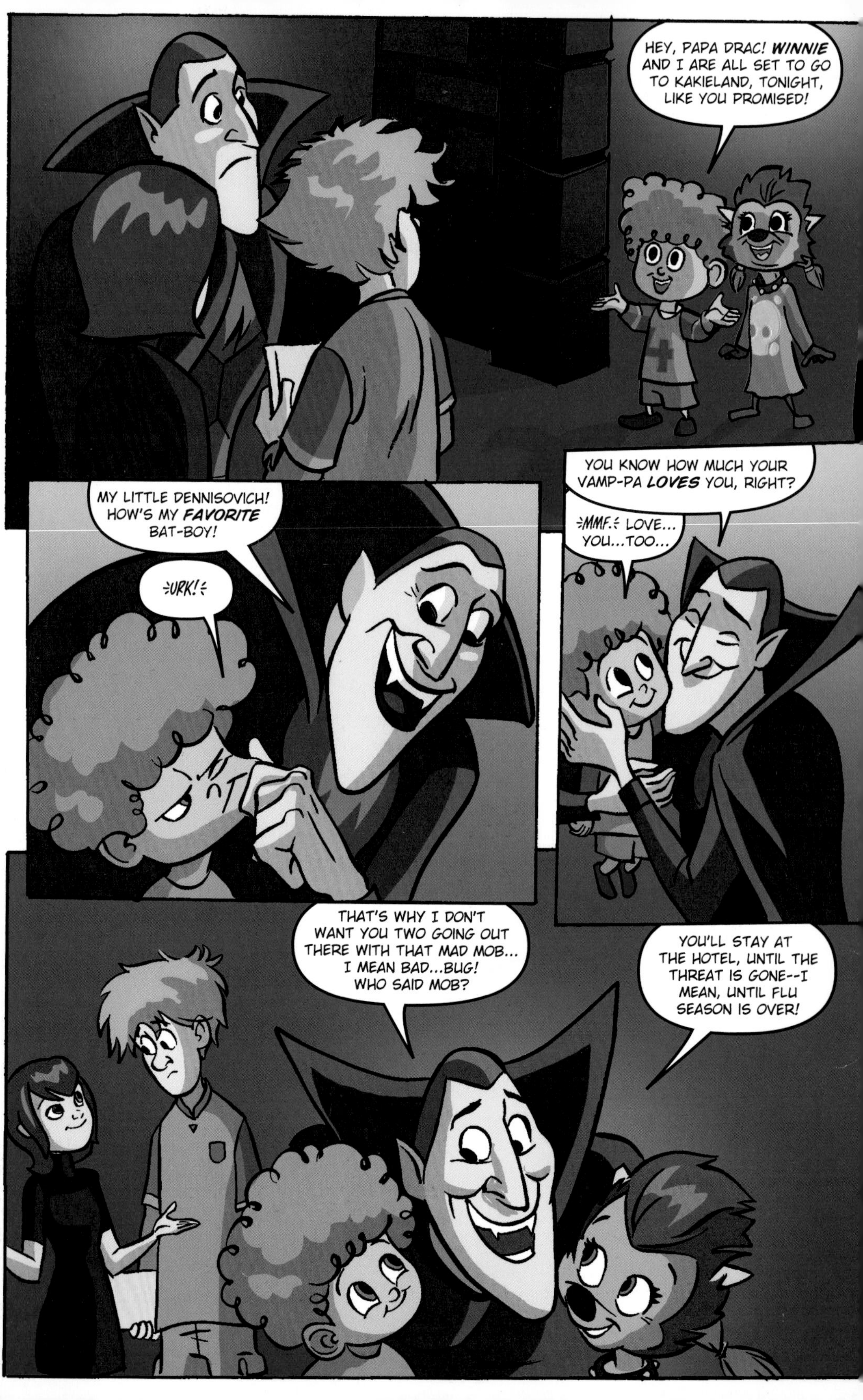
HEY, PAPA DRAC! WINNIE AND I ARE ALL SET TO GO TO KAKIELAND, TONIGHT, LIKE YOU PROMISED!
MY LITTLE DENNISOVICH! HOW'S MY FAVORITE BAT-BOY!
URK!
YOU KNOW HOW MUCH YOUR VAMP-PA LOVES YOU, RIGHT?
MMF. LOVE... YOU...TOO...
THAT'S WHY I DON'T WANT YOU TWO GOING OUT THERE WITH THAT MAD MOB... I MEAN BAD...BUG! WHO SAID MOB?
YOU'LL STAY AT THE HOTEL, UNTIL THE THREAT IS GONE--I MEAN, UNTIL FLU SEASON IS OVER!

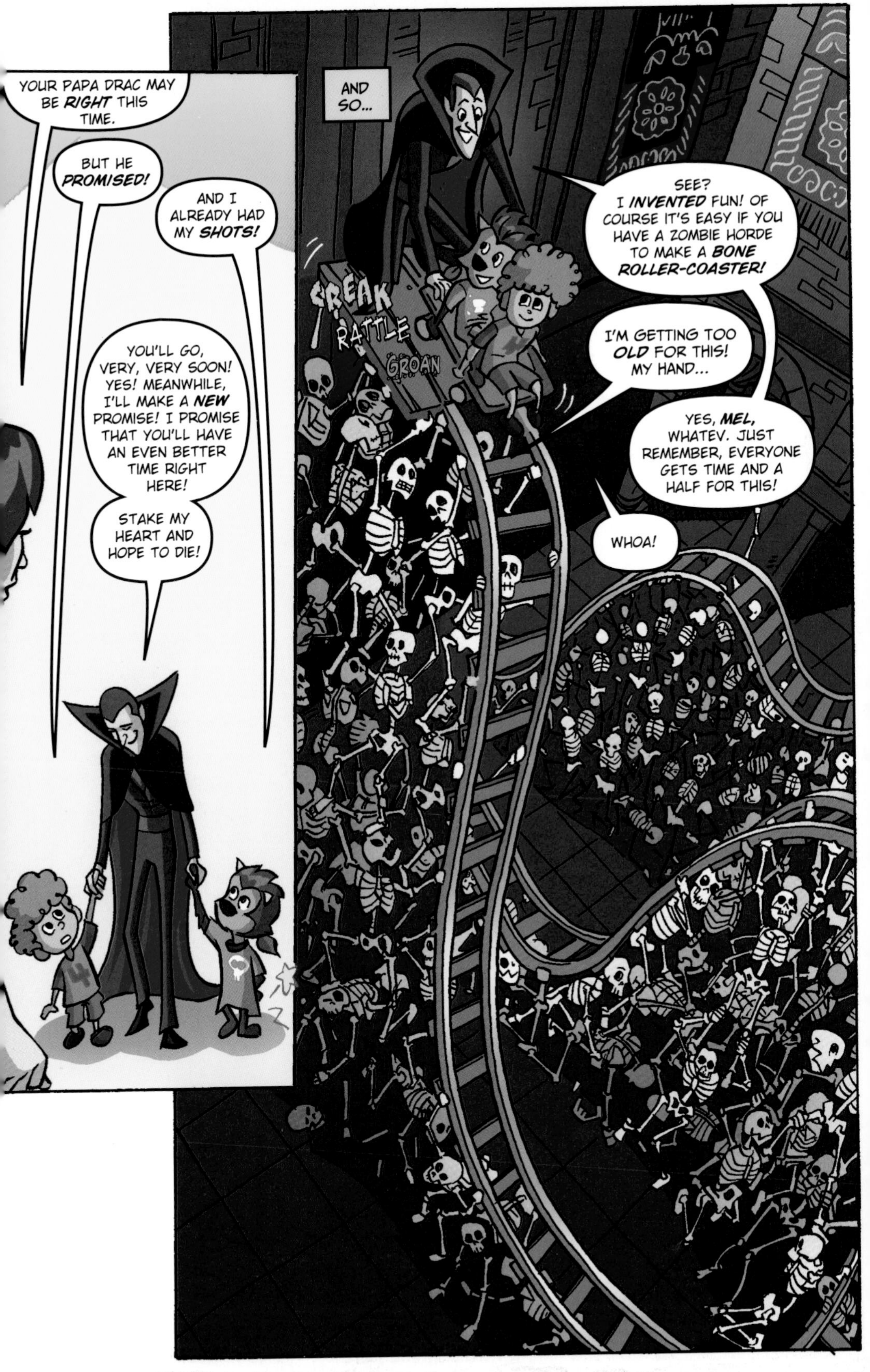
YOUR PAPA DRAC MAY BE RIGHT THIS TIME.
BUT HE PROMISED!
AND I ALREADY HAD MY SHOTS!
YOU'LL GO, VERY, VERY SOON! YES! MEANWHILE, I'LL MAKE A NEW PROMISE! I PROMISE THAT YOU'LL HAVE AN EVEN BETTER TIME RIGHT HERE!
STAKE MY HEART AND HOPE TO DIE!
AND SO...
SEE? I INVENTED FUN! OF COURSE IT'S EASY IF YOU HAVE A ZOMBIE HORDE TO MAKE A BONE ROLLER-COASTER!
CREAK
RATTLE
GROAN
I'M GETTING TOO OLD FOR THIS! MY HAND...
YES, MEL, WHATEV. JUST REMEMBER, EVERYONE GETS TIME AND A HALF FOR THIS!
WHOA!

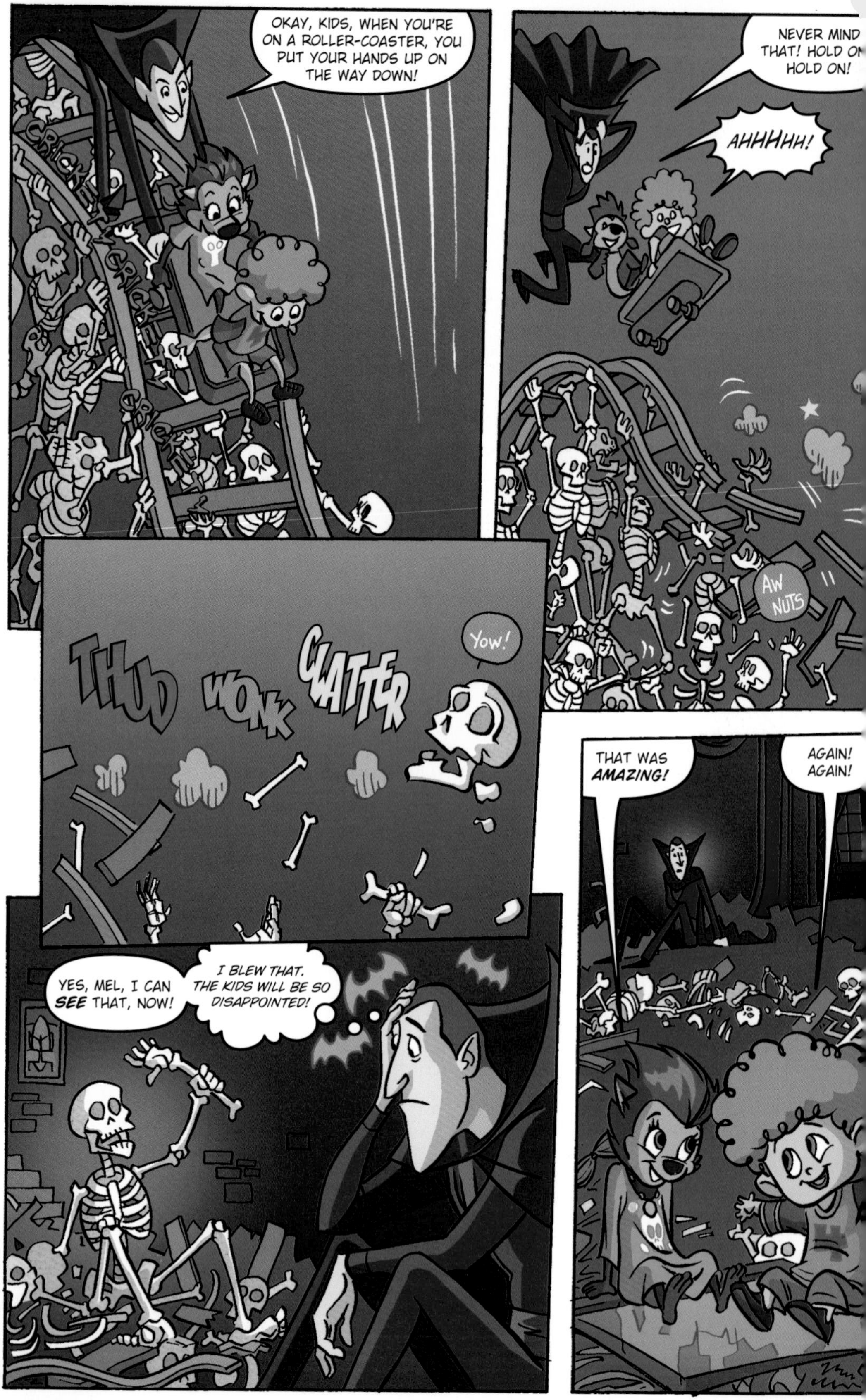

OKAY, KIDS, WHEN YOU'RE ON A ROLLER-COASTER, YOU PUT YOUR HANDS UP ON THE WAY DOWN!
CRICK
CRICK
CRICK
CRICK
NEVER MIND THAT! HOLD ON HOLD ON!
AHHHHH!
AW NUTS
THUD
WONK
CLATTER
YOW!
YES, MEL, I CAN SEE THAT, NOW!
I BLEW THAT. THE KIDS WILL BE SO DISAPPOINTED!
THAT WAS AMAZING!
AGAIN! AGAIN!

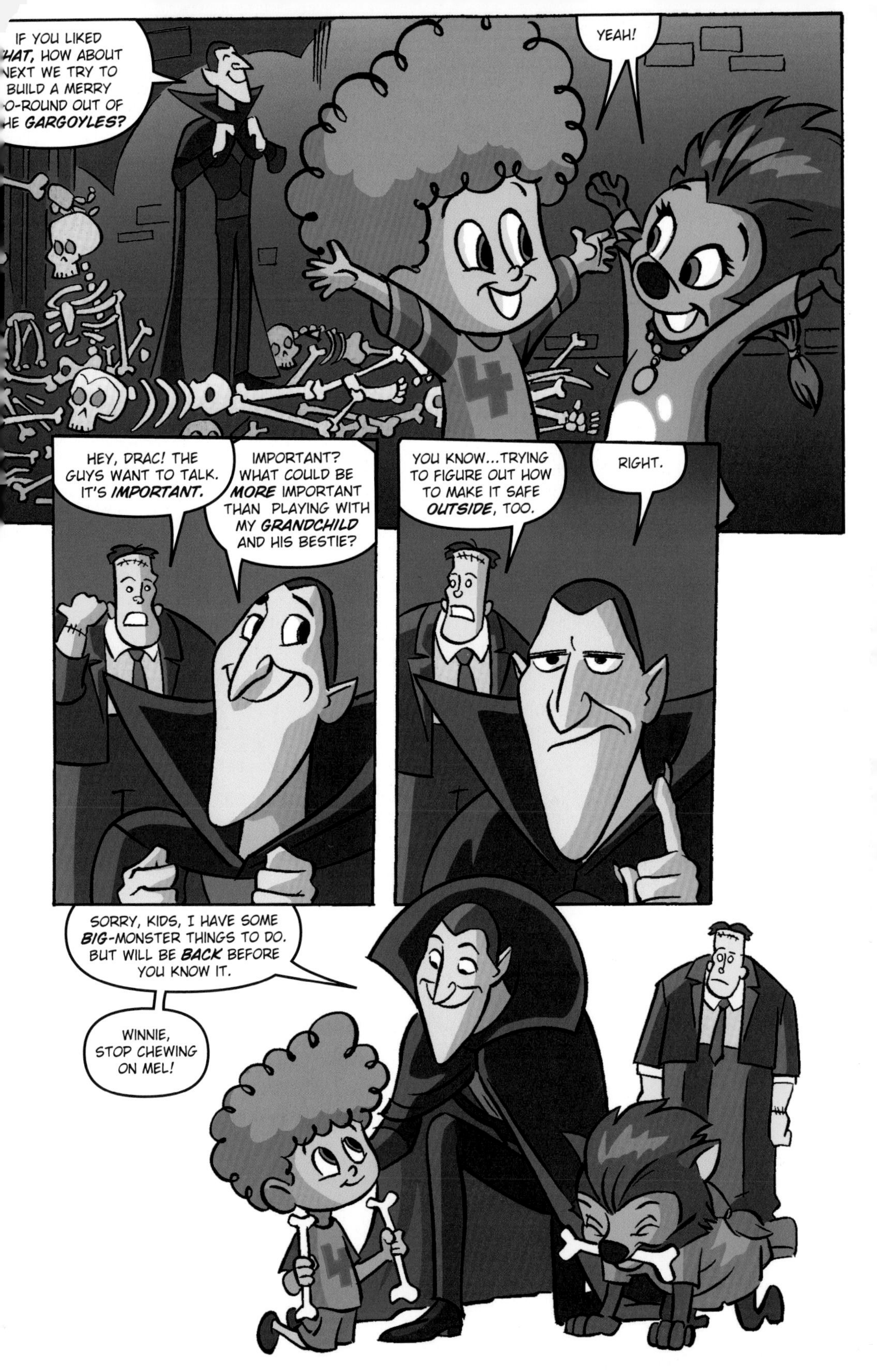
IF YOU LIKED THAT, HOW ABOUT NEXT WE TRY TO BUILD A MERRY GO-ROUND OUT OF THE GARGOYLES?
YEAH!
HEY, DRAC! THE GUYS WANT TO TALK. IT'S IMPORTANT.
IMPORTANT? WHAT COULD BE MORE IMPORTANT THAN PLAYING WITH MY GRANDCHILD AND HIS BESTIE?
YOU KNOW...TRYING TO FIGURE OUT HOW TO MAKE IT SAFE OUTSIDE, TOO.
RIGHT.
SORRY, KIDS, I HAVE SOME BIG-MONSTER THINGS TO DO. BUT WILL BE BACK BEFORE YOU KNOW IT.
WINNIE, STOP CHEWING ON MEL!

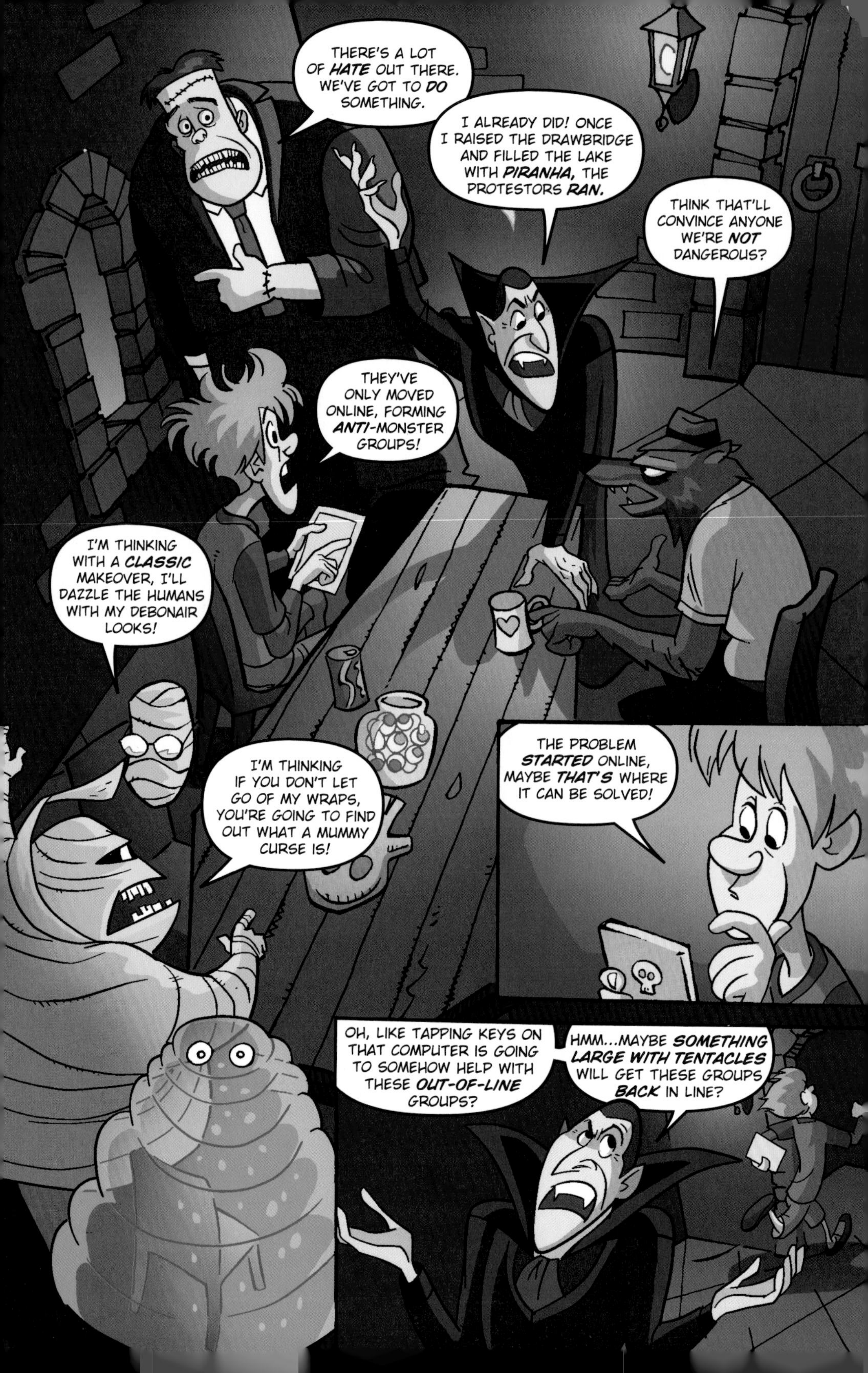
THERE'S A LOT OF HATE OUT THERE. WE'VE GOT TO DO SOMETHING.
I ALREADY DID! ONCE I RAISED THE DRAWBRIDGE AND FILLED THE LAKE WITH PIRANHA, THE PROTESTORS RAN.
THINK THAT'LL CONVINCE ANYONE WE'RE NOT DANGEROUS?
THEY'VE ONLY MOVED ONLINE, FORMING ANTI-MONSTER GROUPS!
I'M THINKING WITH A CLASSIC MAKEOVER, I'LL DAZZLE THE HUMANS WITH MY DEBONAIR LOOKS!
I'M THINKING IF YOU DON'T LET GO OF MY WRAPS, YOU'RE GOING TO FIND OUT WHAT A MUMMY CURSE IS!
THE PROBLEM STARTED ONLINE, MAYBE THAT'S WHERE IT CAN BE SOLVED!
OH, LIKE TAPPING KEYS ON THAT COMPUTER IS GOING TO SOMEHOW HELP WITH THESE OUT-OF-LINE GROUPS?
HMM...MAYBE SOMETHING LARGE WITH TENTACLES WILL GET THESE GROUPS BACK IN LINE?

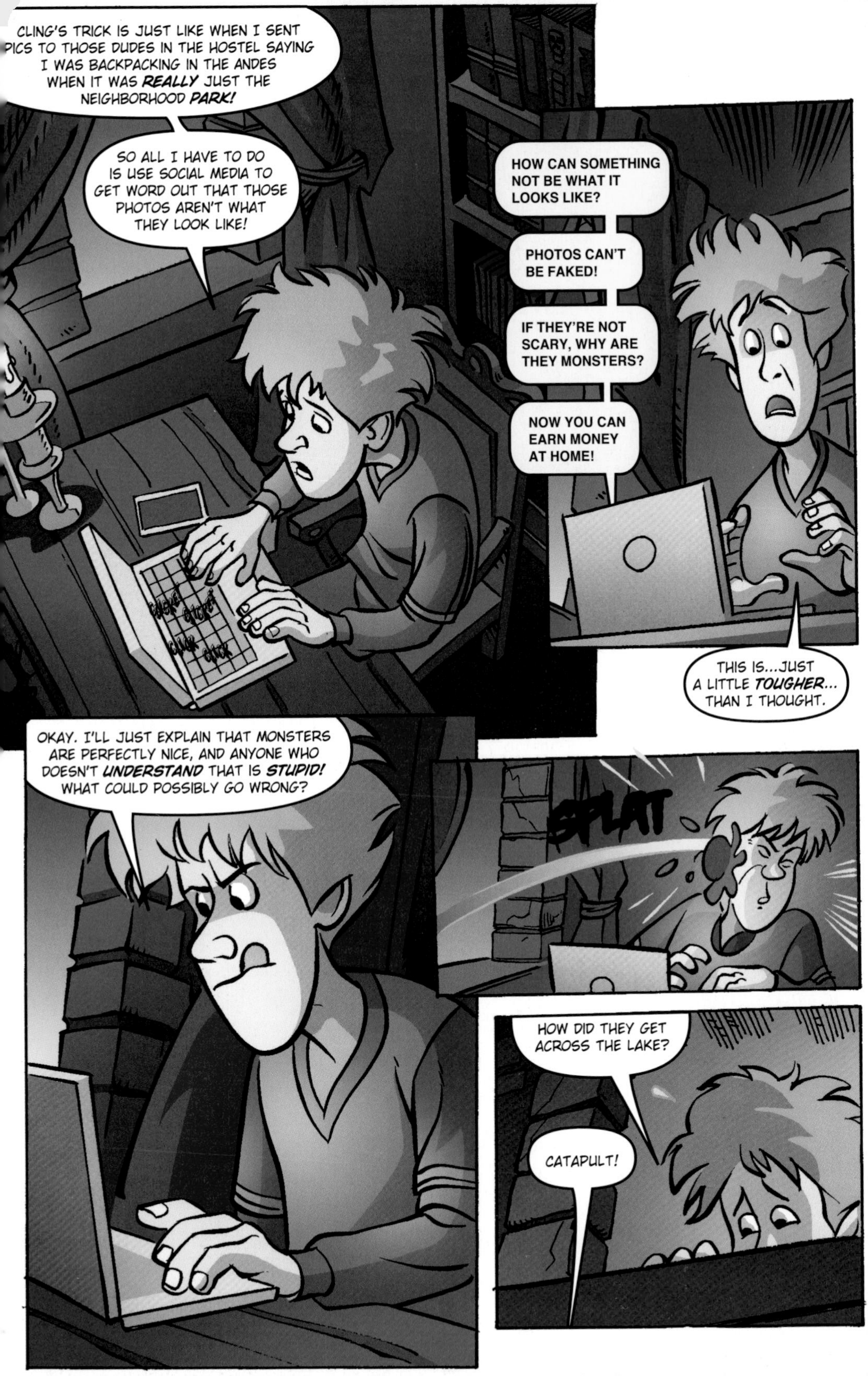
CLING'S TRICK IS JUST LIKE WHEN I SENT PICS TO THOSE DUDES IN THE HOSTEL SAYING I WAS BACKPACKING IN THE ANDES WHEN IT WAS REALLY JUST THE NEIGHBORHOOD PARK!
SO ALL I HAVE TO DO IS USE SOCIAL MEDIA TO GET WORD OUT THAT THOSE PHOTOS AREN'T WHAT THEY LOOK LIKE!
HOW CAN SOMETHING NOT BE WHAT IT LOOKS LIKE?
PHOTOS CAN'T BE FAKED!
IF THEY'RE NOT SCARY, WHY ARE THEY MONSTERS?
NOW YOU CAN EARN MONEY AT HOME!
THIS IS...JUST A LITTLE TOUGHER... THAN I THOUGHT.
OKAY. I'LL JUST EXPLAIN THAT MONSTERS ARE PERFECTLY NICE, AND ANYONE WHO DOESN'T UNDERSTAND THAT IS STUPID! WHAT COULD POSSIBLY GO WRONG?
SPLAT
HOW DID THEY GET ACROSS THE LAKE?
CATAPULT!

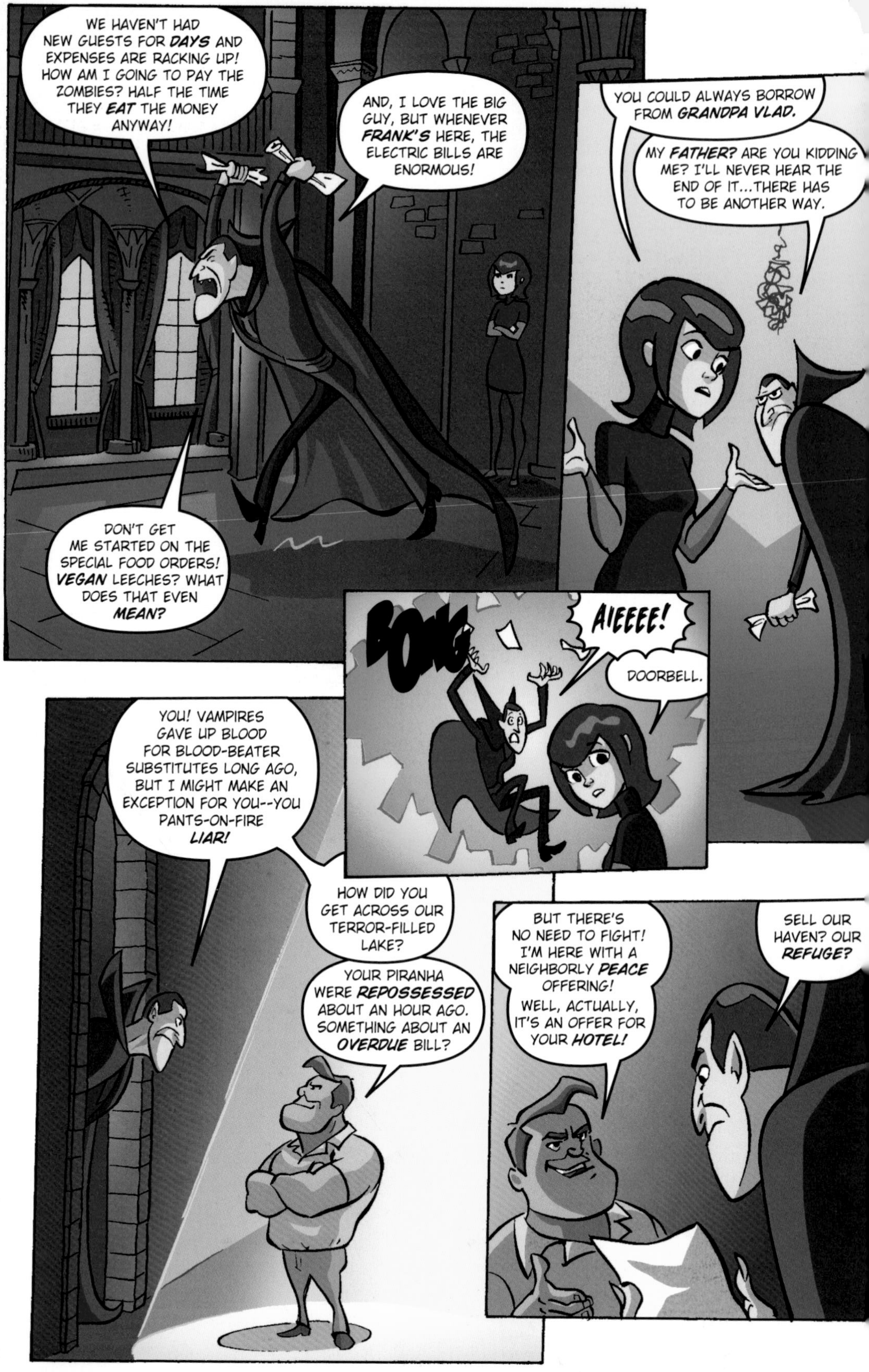
WE HAVEN'T HAD NEW GUESTS FOR DAYS AND EXPENSES ARE RACKING UP! HOW AM I GOING TO PAY THE ZOMBIES? HALF THE TIME THEY EAT THE MONEY ANYWAY!
AND, I LOVE THE BIG GUY, BUT WHENEVER FRANK'S HERE, THE ELECTRIC BILLS ARE ENORMOUS!
DON'T GET ME STARTED ON THE SPECIAL FOOD ORDERS! VEGAN LEECHES? WHAT DOES THAT EVEN MEAN?
YOU COULD ALWAYS BORROW FROM GRANDPA VLAD.
MY FATHER? ARE YOU KIDDING ME? I'LL NEVER HEAR THE END OF IT...THERE HAS TO BE ANOTHER WAY.
BONG
AIEEEE!
DOORBELL.
YOU! VAMPIRES GAVE UP BLOOD FOR BLOOD-BEATER SUBSTITUTES LONG AGO, BUT I MIGHT MAKE AN EXCEPTION FOR YOU--YOU PANTS-ON-FIRE LIAR!
HOW DID YOU GET ACROSS OUR TERROR-FILLED LAKE?
YOUR PIRANHA WERE REPOSSESSED ABOUT AN HOUR AGO. SOMETHING ABOUT AN OVERDUE BILL?
BUT THERE'S NO NEED TO FIGHT! I'M HERE WITH A NEIGHBORLY PEACE OFFERING!
WELL, ACTUALLY, IT'S AN OFFER FOR YOUR HOTEL!
SELL OUR HAVEN? OUR REFUGE?

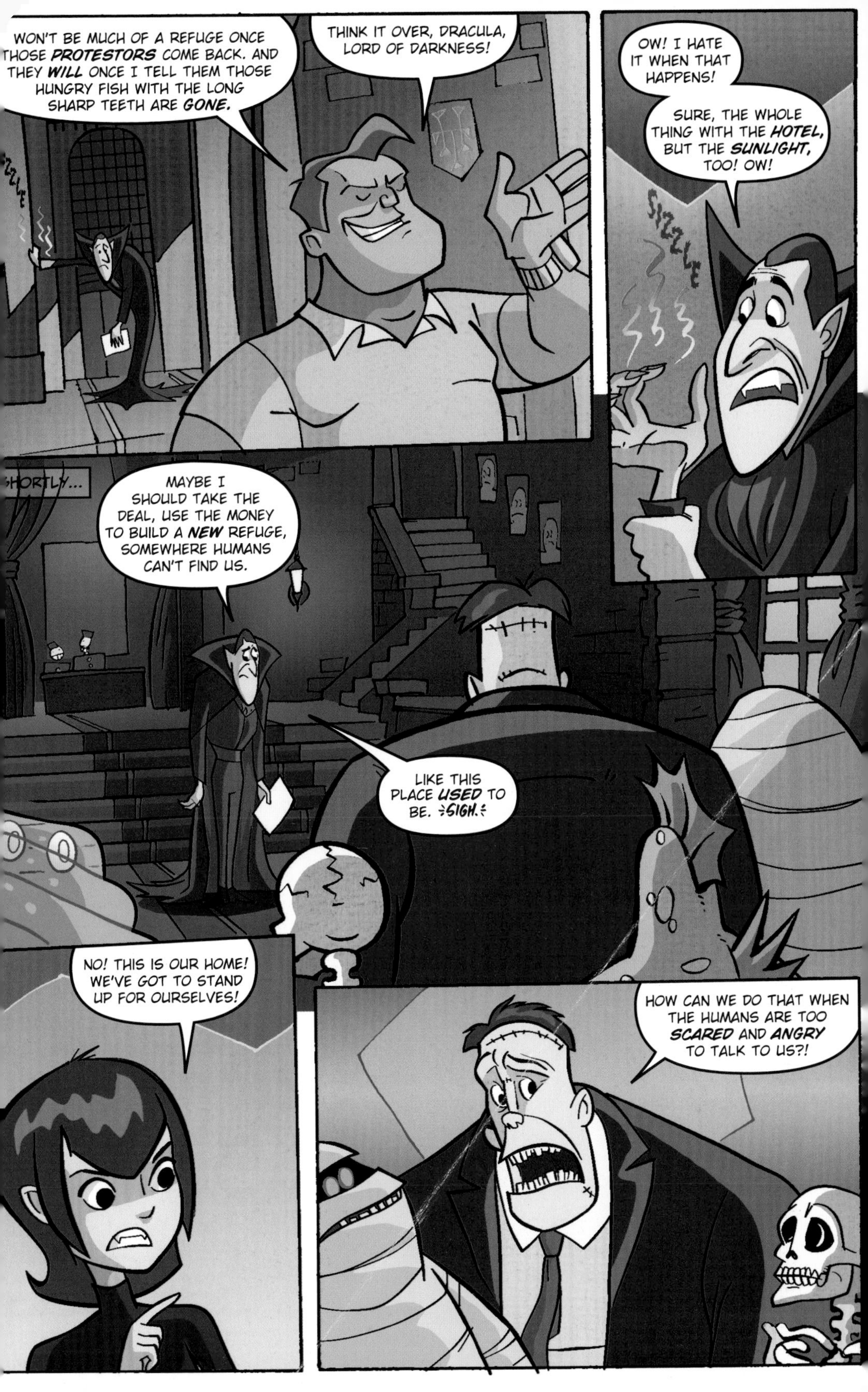
WON'T BE MUCH OF A REFUGE ONCE THOSE PROTESTORS COME BACK. AND THEY WILL ONCE I TELL THEM THOSE HUNGRY FISH WITH THE LONG SHARP TEETH ARE GONE.
THINK IT OVER, DRACULA, LORD OF DARKNESS!
SIZZLE
OW! I HATE IT WHEN THAT HAPPENS!
SURE, THE WHOLE THING WITH THE HOTEL, BUT THE SUNLIGHT, TOO! OW!
SIZZLE
SHORTLY...
MAYBE I SHOULD TAKE THE DEAL, USE THE MONEY TO BUILD A NEW REFUGE, SOMEWHERE HUMANS CAN'T FIND US.
LIKE THIS PLACE USED TO BE. SIGH.
NO! THIS IS OUR HOME! WE'VE GOT TO STAND UP FOR OURSELVES!
HOW CAN WE DO THAT WHEN THE HUMANS ARE TOO SCARED AND ANGRY TO TALK TO US?!

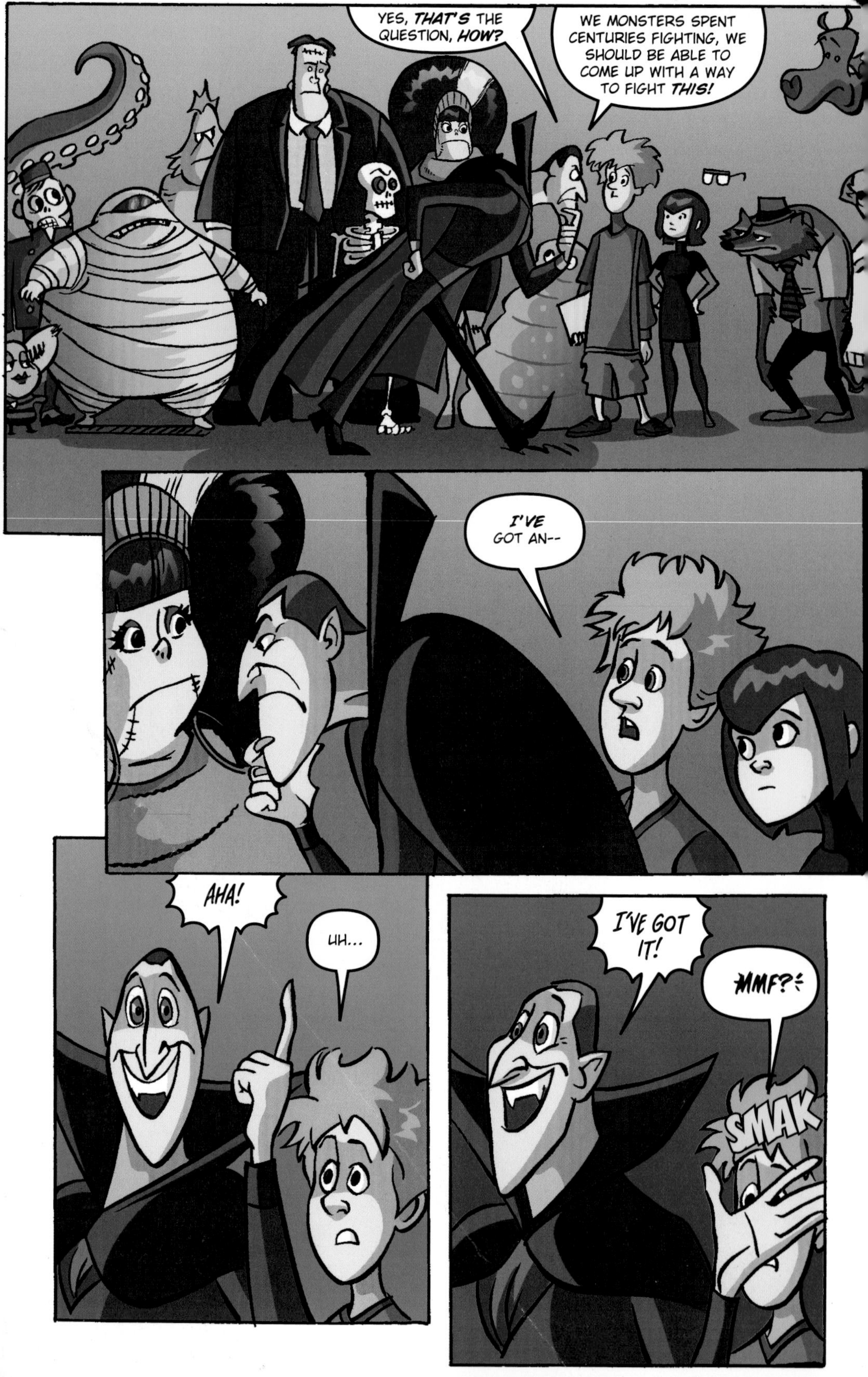
YES, THAT'S THE QUESTION, HOW?
WE MONSTERS SPENT CENTURIES FIGHTING, WE SHOULD BE ABLE TO COME UP WITH A WAY TO FIGHT THIS!
I'VE GOT AN--
AHA!
UH...
I'VE GOT IT!
MMF?
SMAK

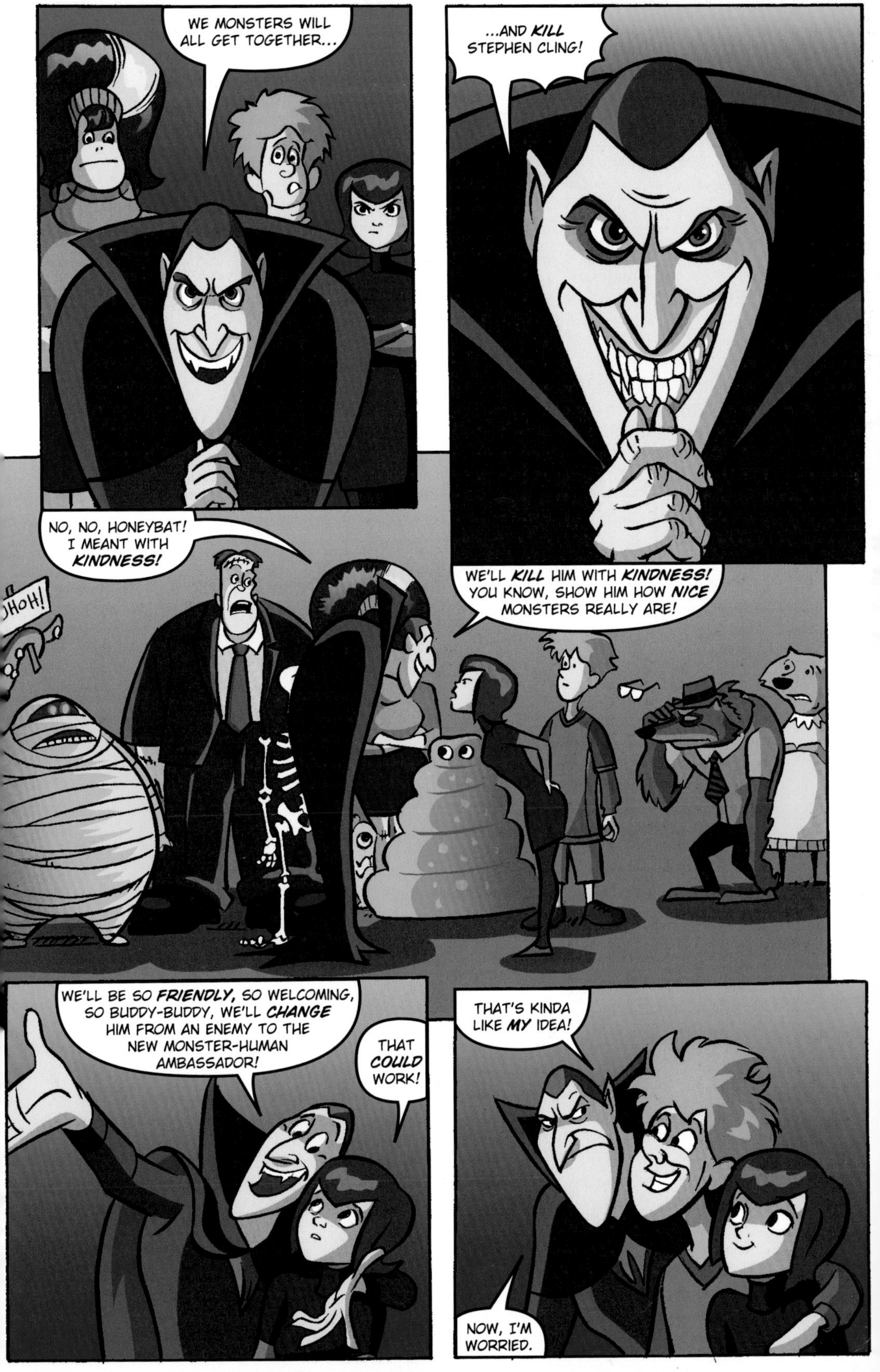

WE MONSTERS WILL ALL GET TOGETHER...
...AND KILL STEPHEN CLING!
NO, NO, HONEYBAT! I MEANT WITH KINDNESS!
UHOH!
WE'LL KILL HIM WITH KINDNESS! YOU KNOW, SHOW HIM HOW NICE MONSTERS REALLY ARE!
WE'LL BE SO FRIENDLY, SO WELCOMING, SO BUDDY-BUDDY, WE'LL CHANGE HIM FROM AN ENEMY TO THE NEW MONSTER-HUMAN AMBASSADOR!
THAT COULD WORK!
THAT'S KINDA LIKE MY IDEA!
NOW, I'M WORRIED.

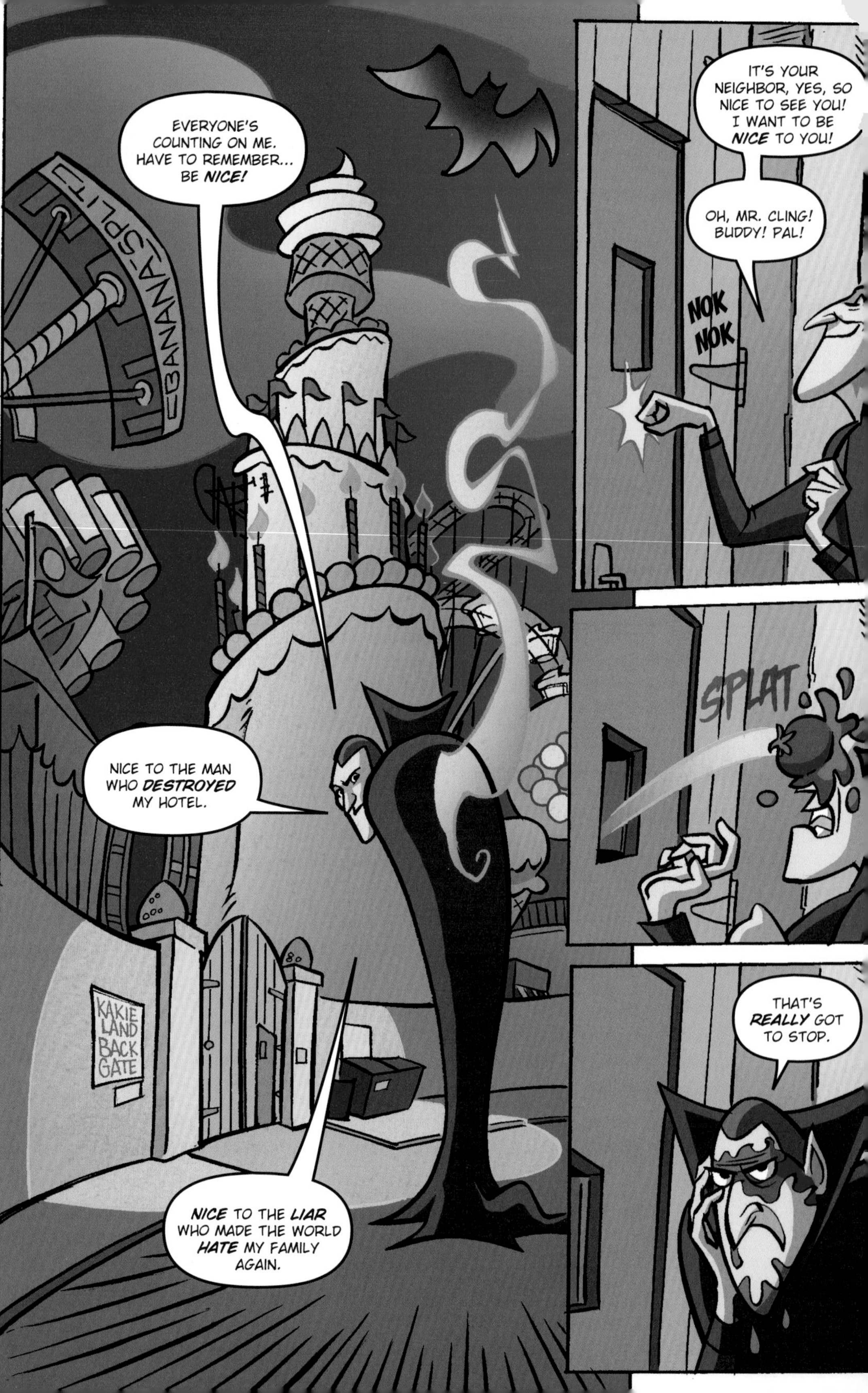
BANANA-SPLIT
EVERYONE'S COUNTING ON ME. HAVE TO REMEMBER... BE NICE!
NICE TO THE MAN WHO DESTROYED MY HOTEL.
KAKIE LAND BACK GATE
NICE TO THE LIAR WHO MADE THE WORLD HATE MY FAMILY AGAIN.
NOK NOK
IT'S YOUR NEIGHBOR, YES, SO NICE TO SEE YOU! I WANT TO BE NICE TO YOU!
OH, MR. CLING! BUDDY! PAL!
SPLAT
THAT'S REALLY GOT TO STOP.

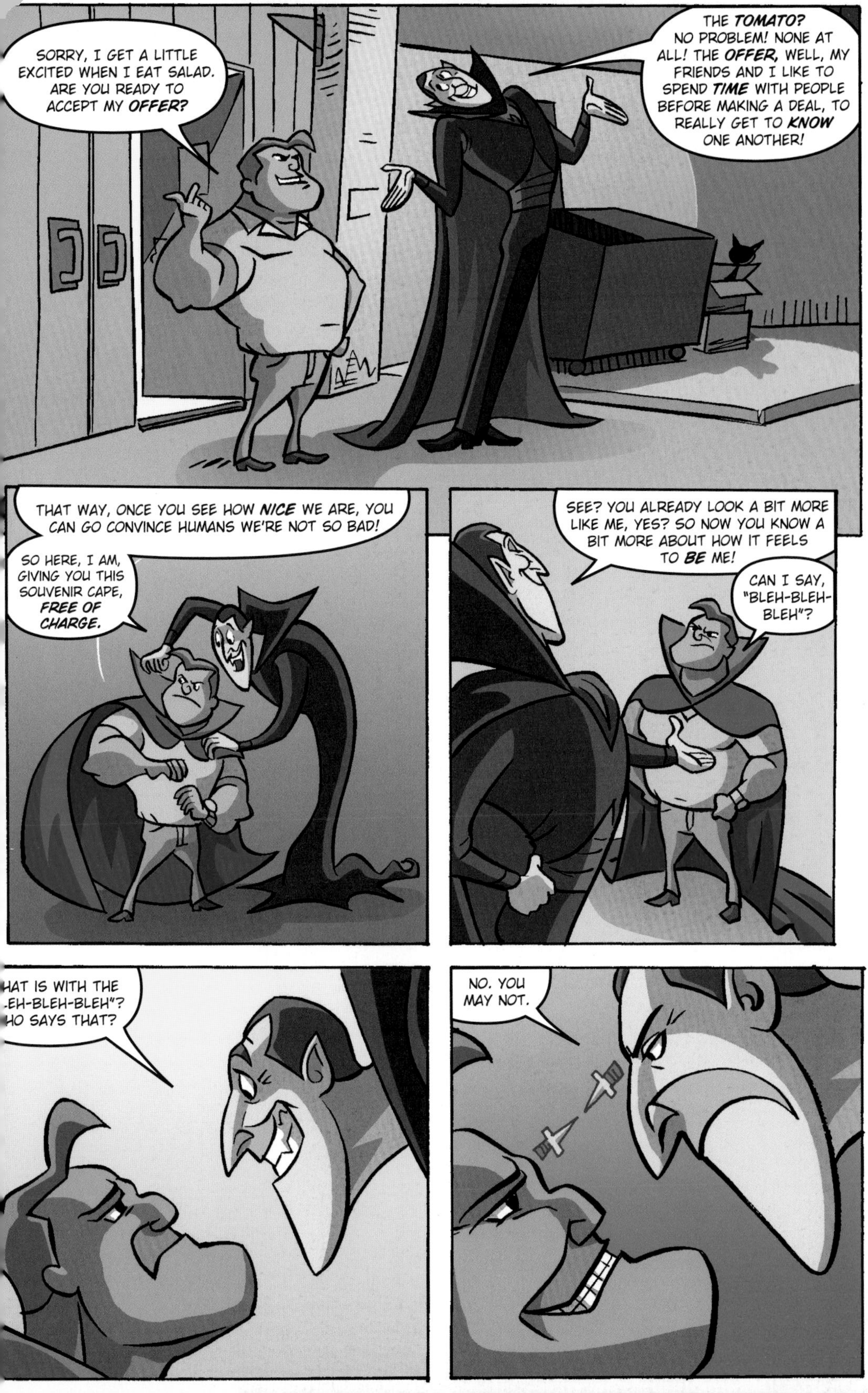
SORRY, I GET A LITTLE EXCITED WHEN I EAT SALAD. ARE YOU READY TO ACCEPT MY ***OFFER?***
THE ***TOMATO?*** NO PROBLEM! NONE AT ALL! THE ***OFFER,*** WELL, MY FRIENDS AND I LIKE TO SPEND ***TIME*** WITH PEOPLE BEFORE MAKING A DEAL, TO REALLY GET TO ***KNOW*** ONE ANOTHER!
THAT WAY, ONCE YOU SEE HOW ***NICE*** WE ARE, YOU CAN GO CONVINCE HUMANS WE'RE NOT SO BAD!
SO HERE, I AM, GIVING YOU THIS SOUVENIR CAPE, ***FREE OF CHARGE.***
SEE? YOU ALREADY LOOK A BIT MORE LIKE ME, YES? SO NOW YOU KNOW A BIT MORE ABOUT HOW IT FEELS TO ***BE*** ME!
CAN I SAY, "BLEH-BLEH-BLEH"?
HAT IS WITH THE
EH-BLEH-BLEH"?
HO SAYS THAT?
NO. YOU MAY NOT.

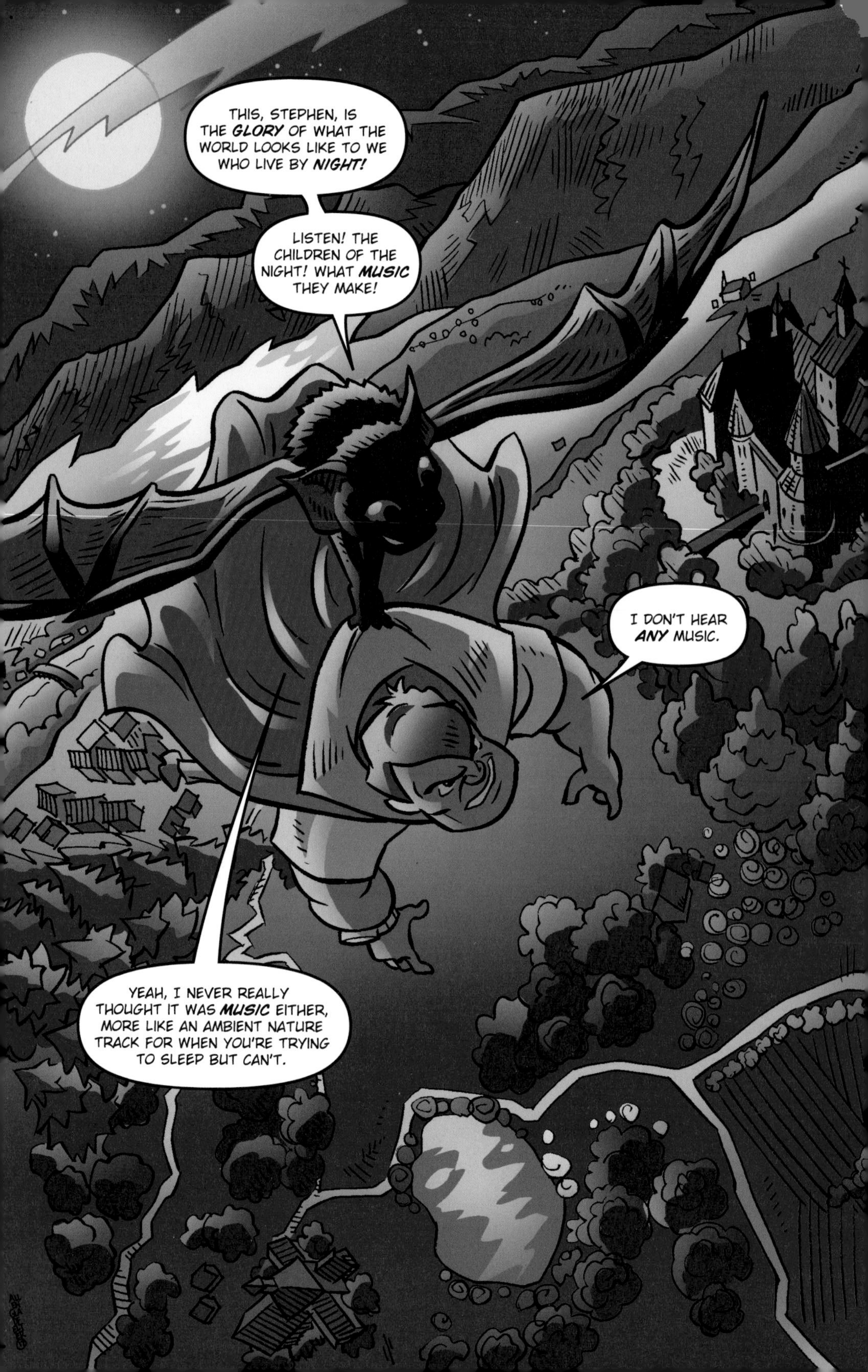
THIS, STEPHEN, IS THE GLORY OF WHAT THE WORLD LOOKS LIKE TO WE WHO LIVE BY NIGHT!
LISTEN! THE CHILDREN OF THE NIGHT! WHAT MUSIC THEY MAKE!
I DON'T HEAR ANY MUSIC.
YEAH, I NEVER REALLY THOUGHT IT WAS MUSIC EITHER, MORE LIKE AN AMBIENT NATURE TRACK FOR WHEN YOU'RE TRYING TO SLEEP BUT CAN'T.

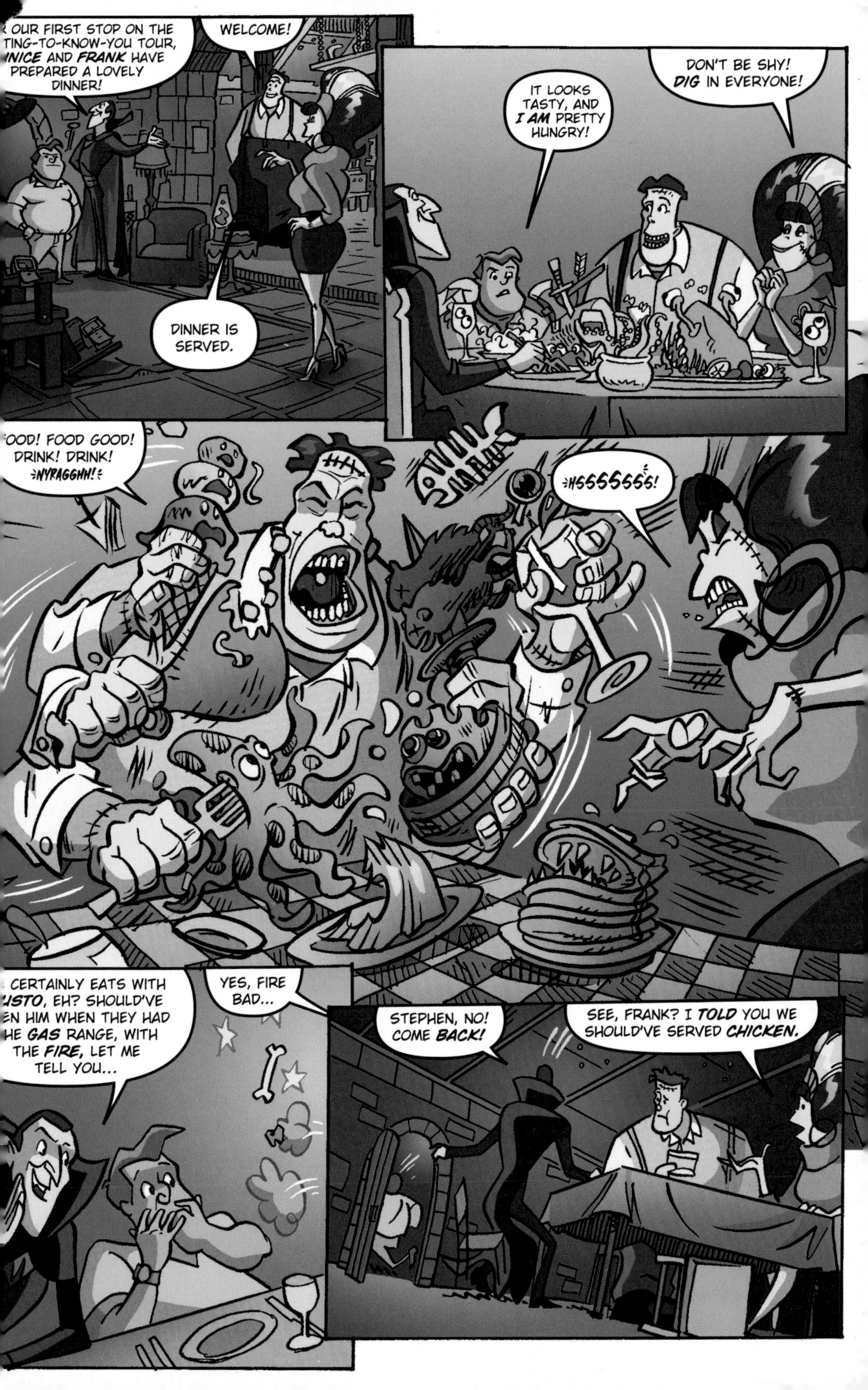

R OUR FIRST STOP ON THE TING-TO-KNOW-YOU TOUR, NICE AND FRANK HAVE PREPARED A LOVELY DINNER!
WELCOME!
DINNER IS SERVED.
IT LOOKS TASTY, AND I AM PRETTY HUNGRY!
DON'T BE SHY! DIG IN EVERYONE!
OOD! FOOD GOOD! DRINK! DRINK! NYRAGGHH!
HSSSSSSS!
E CERTAINLY EATS WITH USTO, EH? SHOULD'VE EN HIM WHEN THEY HAD HE GAS RANGE, WITH THE FIRE, LET ME TELL YOU...
YES, FIRE BAD...
STEPHEN, NO! COME BACK!
SEE, FRANK? I TOLD YOU WE SHOULD'VE SERVED CHICKEN.

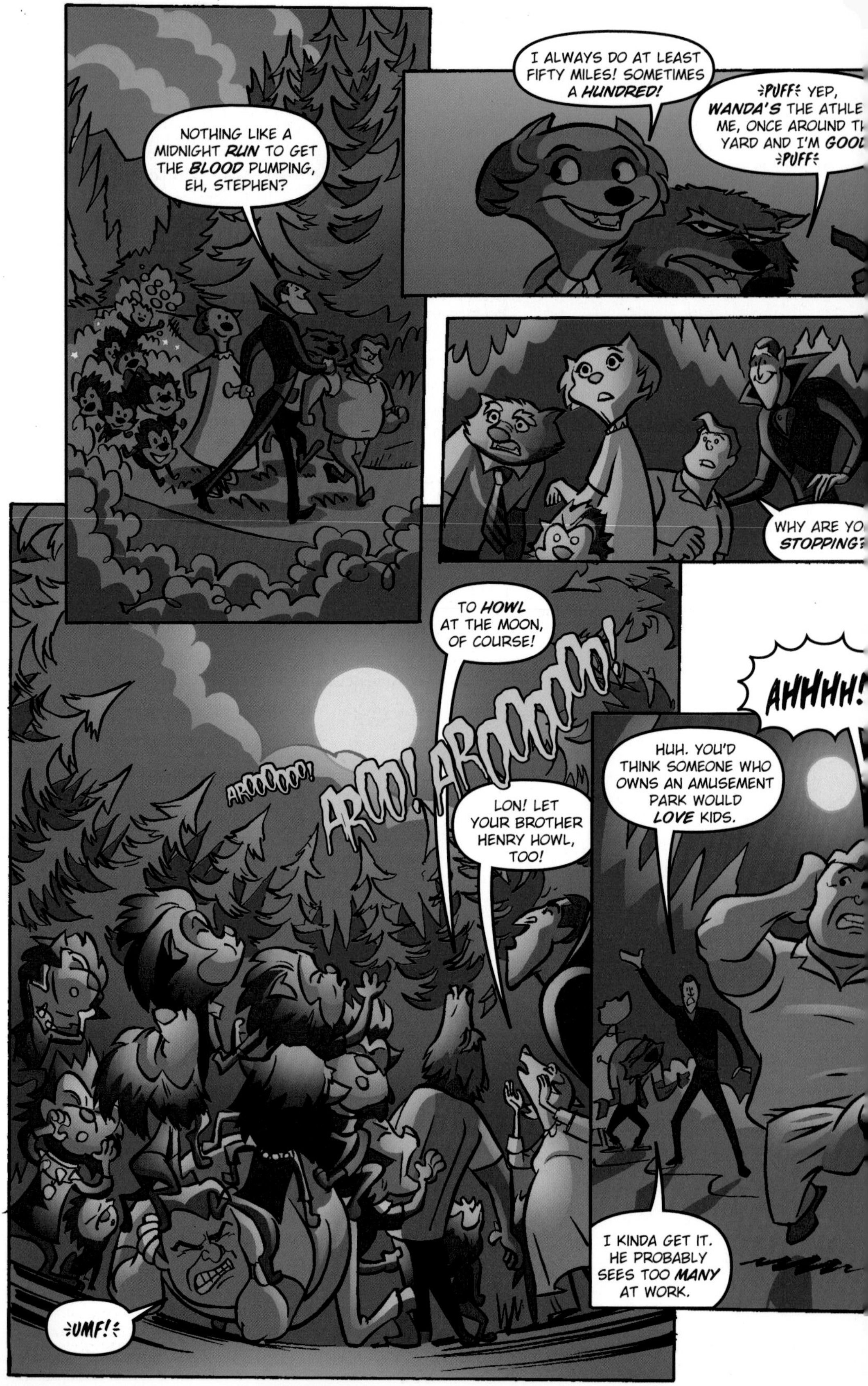

NOTHING LIKE A MIDNIGHT *RUN* TO GET THE *BLOOD* PUMPING, EH, STEPHEN?
I ALWAYS DO AT LEAST FIFTY MILES! SOMETIMES A *HUNDRED!*
PUFF YEP, *WANDA'S* THE ATHLE ME, ONCE AROUND T YARD AND I'M *GOOD* *PUFF*
WHY ARE YO *STOPPING?*
TO *HOWL* AT THE MOON, OF COURSE!
AROOOOOO!
AROO! AROOOOOO!
LON! LET YOUR BROTHER HENRY HOWL, TOO!
UMF!
AHHHH!
HUH. YOU'D THINK SOMEONE WHO OWNS AN AMUSEMENT PARK WOULD *LOVE* KIDS.
I KINDA GET IT. HE PROBABLY SEES TOO *MANY* AT WORK.

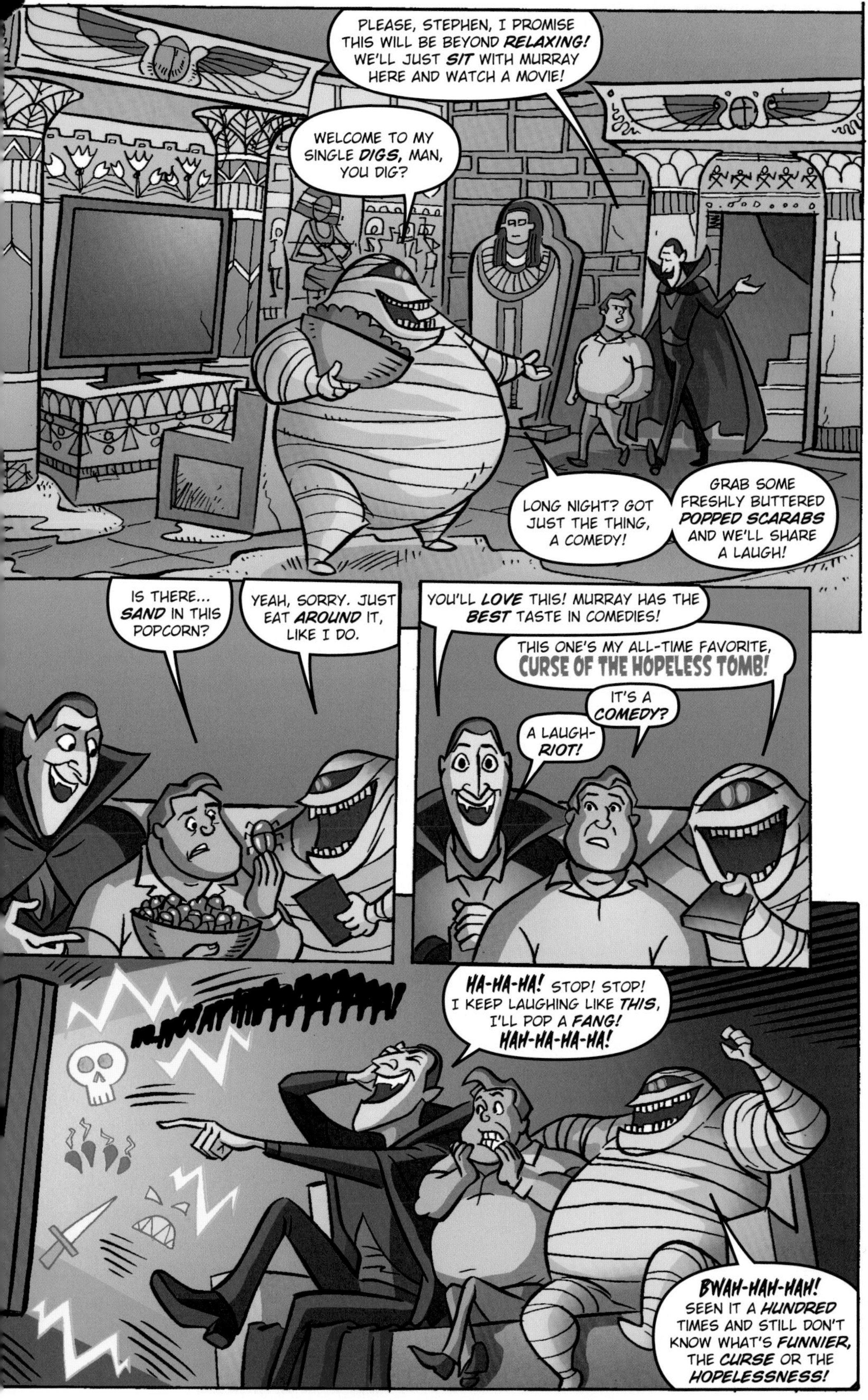
PLEASE, STEPHEN, I PROMISE THIS WILL BE BEYOND *RELAXING!* WE'LL JUST *SIT* WITH MURRAY HERE AND WATCH A MOVIE!
WELCOME TO MY SINGLE *DIGS,* MAN, YOU DIG?
LONG NIGHT? GOT JUST THE THING, A COMEDY!
GRAB SOME FRESHLY BUTTERED *POPPED SCARABS* AND WE'LL SHARE A LAUGH!
IS THERE... *SAND* IN THIS POPCORN?
YEAH, SORRY. JUST EAT *AROUND* IT, LIKE I DO.
YOU'LL *LOVE* THIS! MURRAY HAS THE *BEST* TASTE IN COMEDIES!
THIS ONE'S MY ALL-TIME FAVORITE, CURSE OF THE HOPELESS TOMB!
IT'S A *COMEDY?*
A LAUGH-*RIOT!*
HA-HA-HA! STOP! STOP! I KEEP LAUGHING LIKE *THIS,* I'LL POP A *FANG!* *HAH-HA-HA-HA!*
BWAH-HAH-HAH! SEEN IT A *HUNDRED* TIMES AND STILL DON'T KNOW WHAT'S *FUNNIER,* THE *CURSE* OR THE *HOPELESSNESS!*

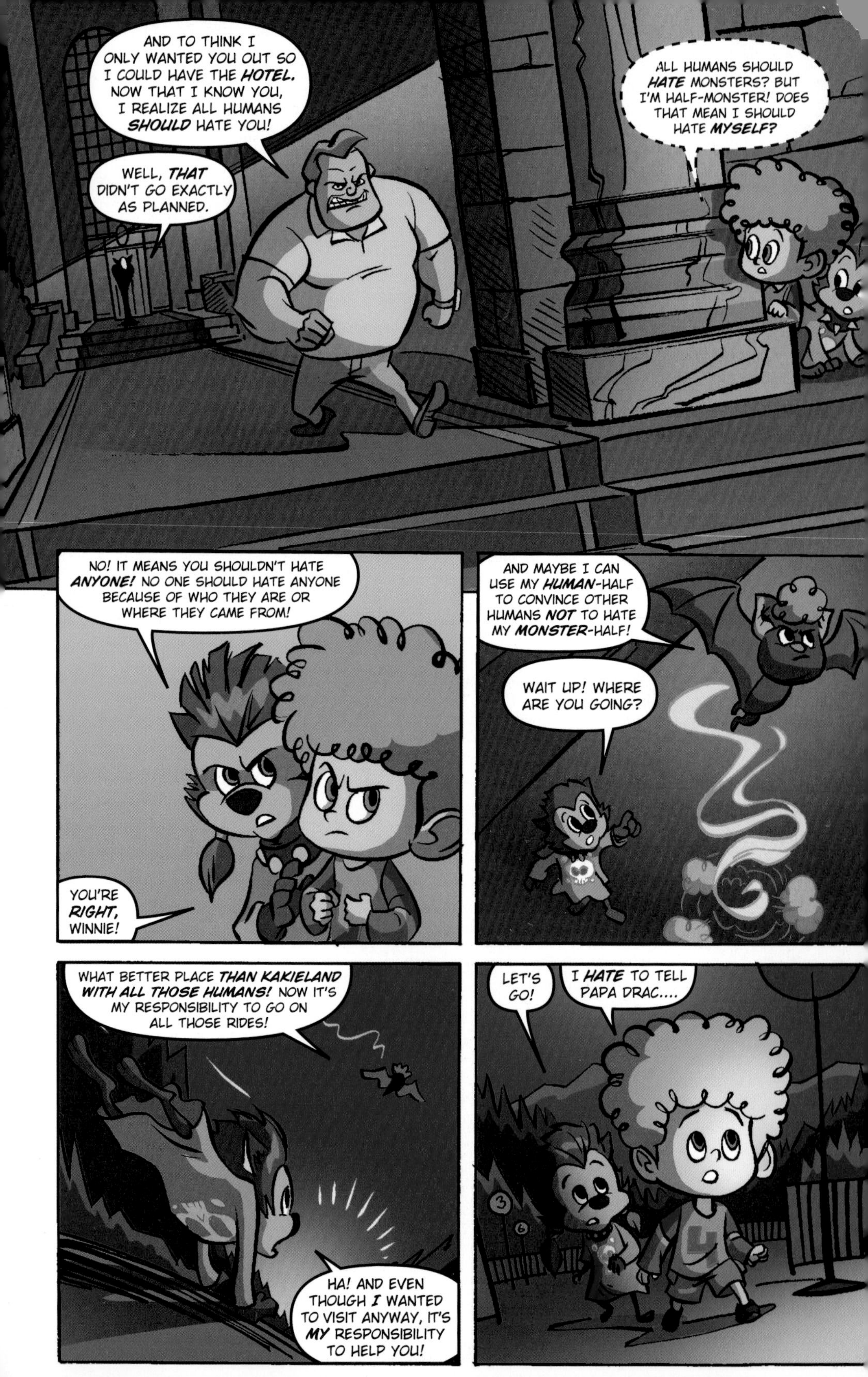
AND TO THINK I ONLY WANTED YOU OUT SO I COULD HAVE THE HOTEL. NOW THAT I KNOW YOU, I REALIZE ALL HUMANS SHOULD HATE YOU!
WELL, THAT DIDN'T GO EXACTLY AS PLANNED.
ALL HUMANS SHOULD HATE MONSTERS? BUT I'M HALF-MONSTER! DOES THAT MEAN I SHOULD HATE MYSELF?
NO! IT MEANS YOU SHOULDN'T HATE ANYONE! NO ONE SHOULD HATE ANYONE BECAUSE OF WHO THEY ARE OR WHERE THEY CAME FROM!
YOU'RE RIGHT, WINNIE!
AND MAYBE I CAN USE MY HUMAN-HALF TO CONVINCE OTHER HUMANS NOT TO HATE MY MONSTER-HALF!
WAIT UP! WHERE ARE YOU GOING?
WHAT BETTER PLACE THAN KAKIELAND WITH ALL THOSE HUMANS! NOW IT'S MY RESPONSIBILITY TO GO ON ALL THOSE RIDES!
HA! AND EVEN THOUGH I WANTED TO VISIT ANYWAY, IT'S MY RESPONSIBILITY TO HELP YOU!
LET'S GO!
I HATE TO TELL PAPA DRAC....

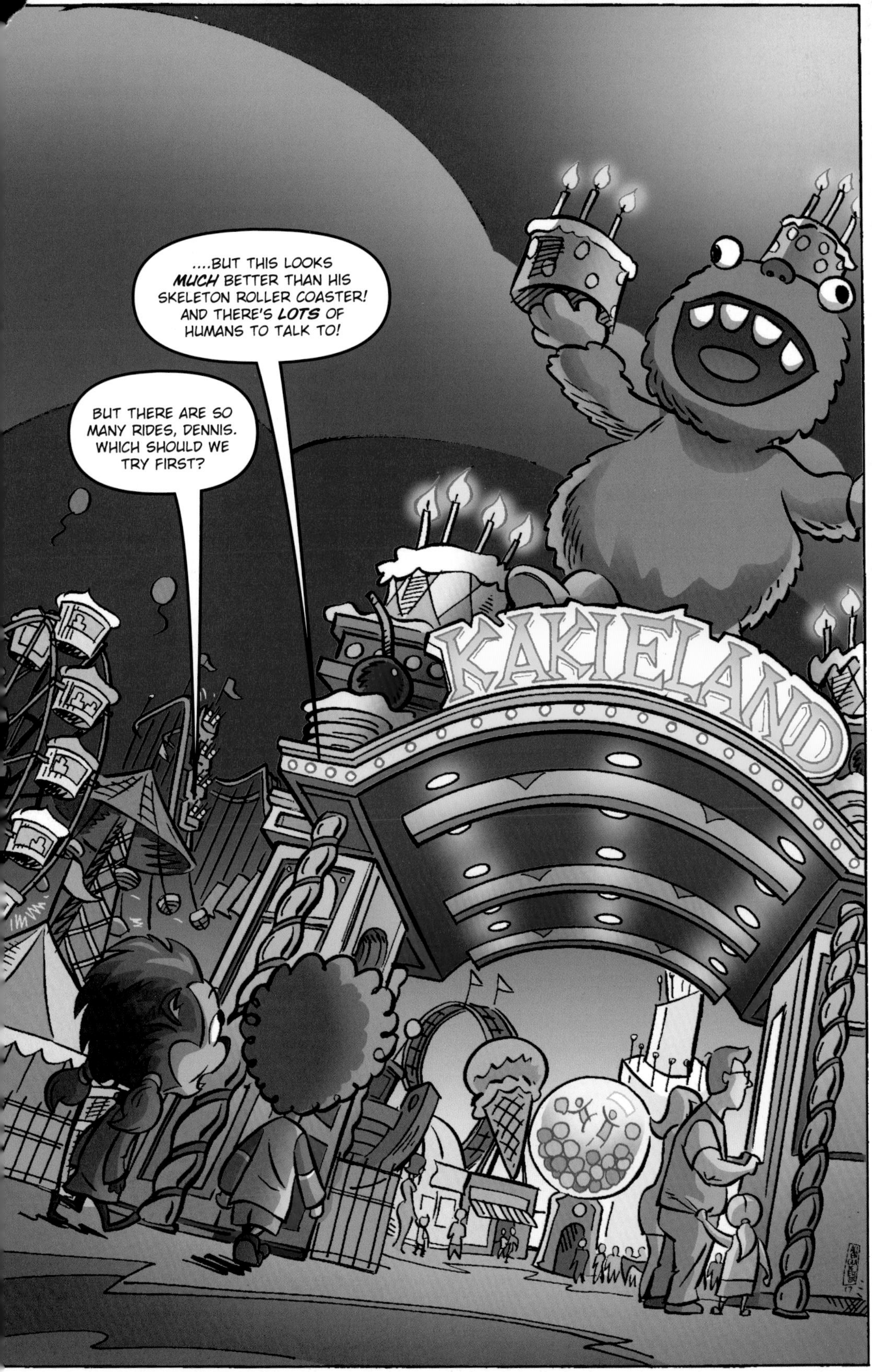
BUT THERE ARE SO MANY RIDES, DENNIS. WHICH SHOULD WE TRY FIRST?
....BUT THIS LOOKS MUCH BETTER THAN HIS SKELETON ROLLER COASTER! AND THERE'S LOTS OF HUMANS TO TALK TO!
KAKIELAND

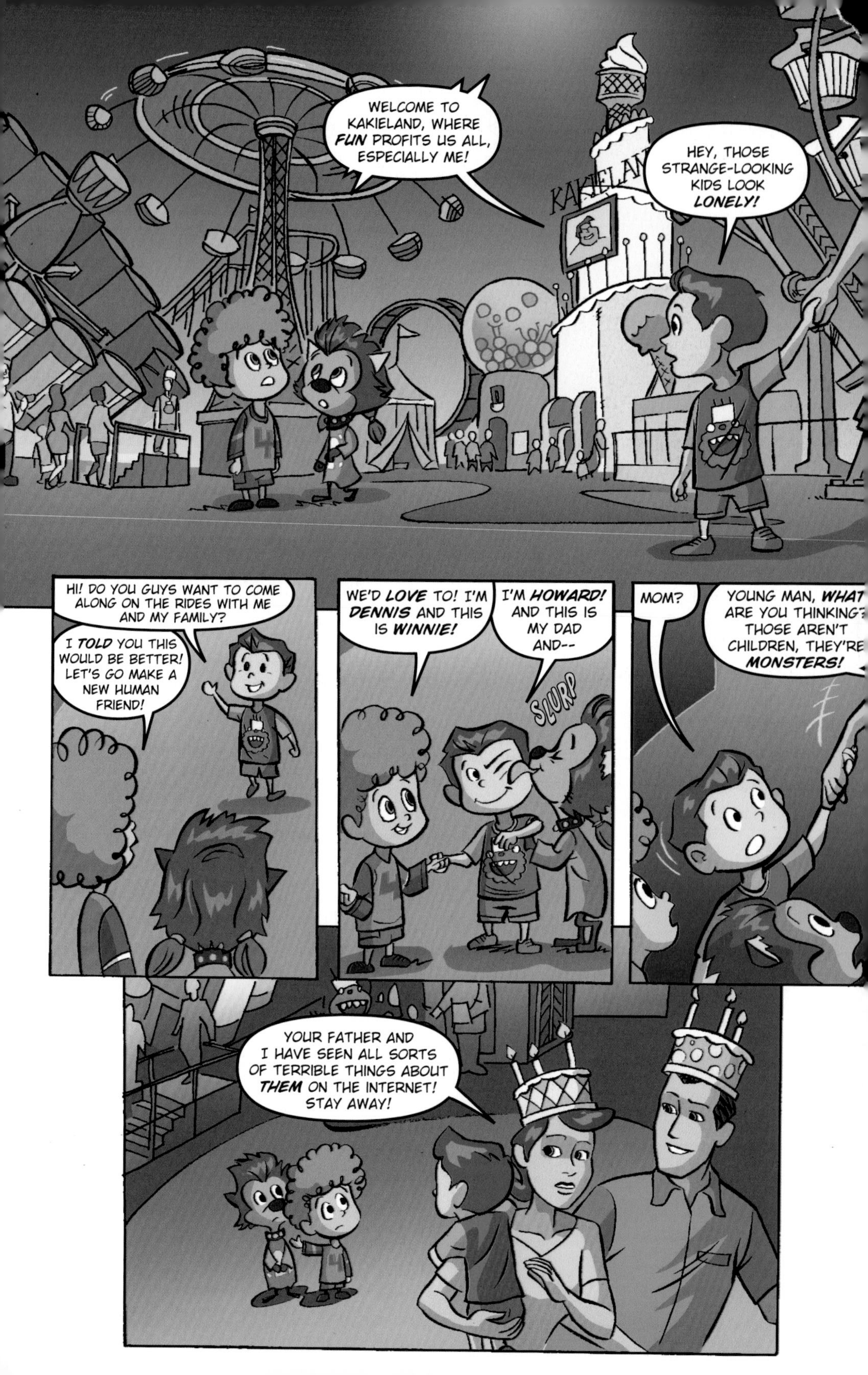
WELCOME TO KAKIELAND, WHERE FUN PROFITS US ALL, ESPECIALLY ME!
HEY, THOSE STRANGE-LOOKING KIDS LOOK LONELY!
KAKIELAND
HI! DO YOU GUYS WANT TO COME ALONG ON THE RIDES WITH ME AND MY FAMILY?
I TOLD YOU THIS WOULD BE BETTER! LET'S GO MAKE A NEW HUMAN FRIEND!
WE'D LOVE TO! I'M DENNIS AND THIS IS WINNIE!
I'M HOWARD! AND THIS IS MY DAD AND--
SLURP
MOM?
YOUNG MAN, WHAT ARE YOU THINKING? THOSE AREN'T CHILDREN, THEY'RE MONSTERS!
YOUR FATHER AND I HAVE SEEN ALL SORTS OF TERRIBLE THINGS ABOUT THEM ON THE INTERNET! STAY AWAY!

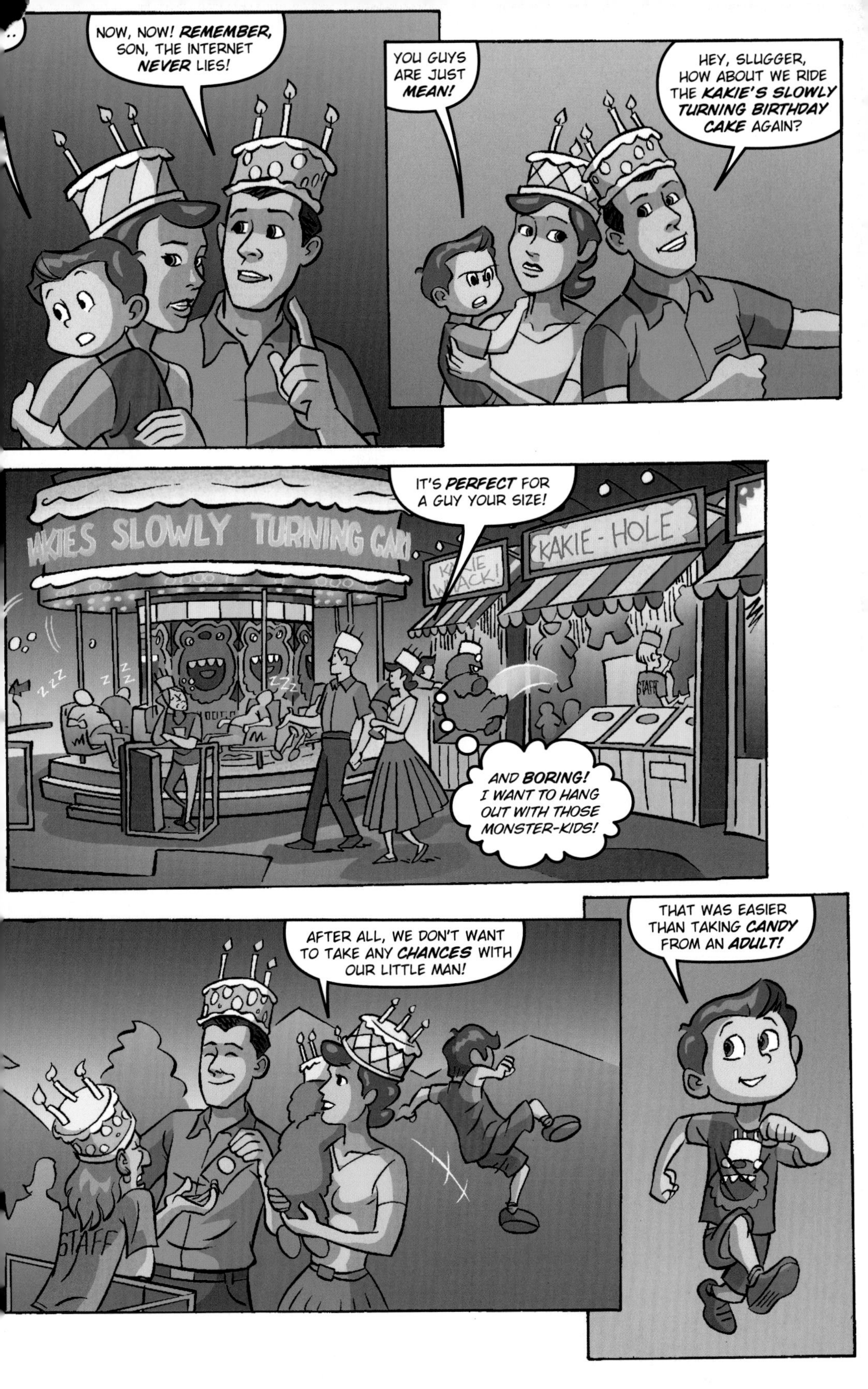

NOW, NOW! REMEMBER, SON, THE INTERNET NEVER LIES!
YOU GUYS ARE JUST MEAN!
HEY, SLUGGER, HOW ABOUT WE RIDE THE KAKIE'S SLOWLY TURNING BIRTHDAY CAKE AGAIN?
KAKIES SLOWLY TURNING CAKE
KAKIE WHACK!
KAKIE - HOLE
IT'S PERFECT FOR A GUY YOUR SIZE!
AND BORING! I WANT TO HANG OUT WITH THOSE MONSTER-KIDS!
STAFF
AFTER ALL, WE DON'T WANT TO TAKE ANY CHANCES WITH OUR LITTLE MAN!
STAFF
THAT WAS EASIER THAN TAKING CANDY FROM AN ADULT!

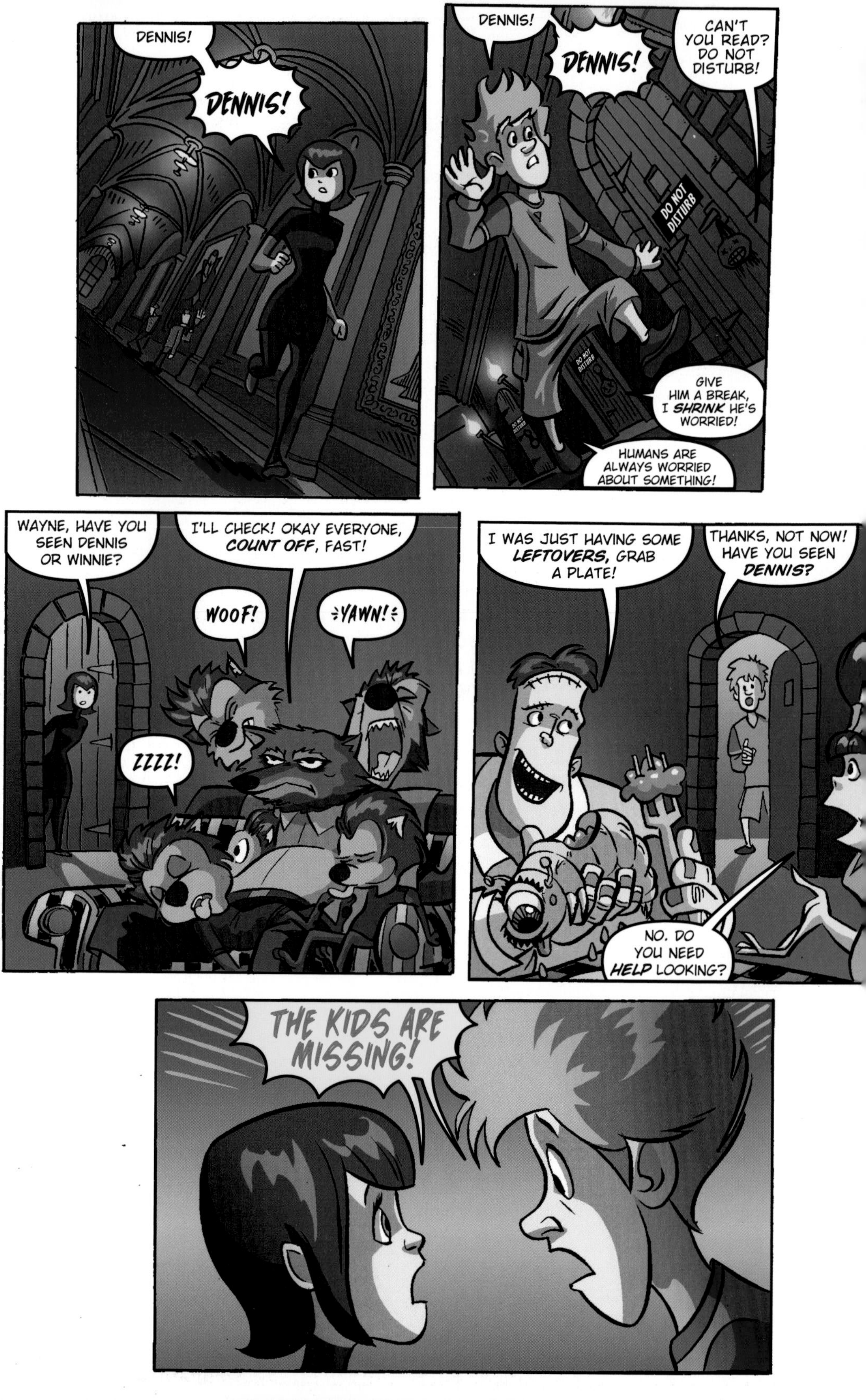
DENNIS!
DENNIS!
DENNIS!
DENNIS!
CAN'T YOU READ? DO NOT DISTURB!
DO NOT DISTURB
DO NOT DISTURB
GIVE HIM A BREAK, I SHRINK HE'S WORRIED!
HUMANS ARE ALWAYS WORRIED ABOUT SOMETHING!
WAYNE, HAVE YOU SEEN DENNIS OR WINNIE?
I'LL CHECK! OKAY EVERYONE, COUNT OFF, FAST!
WOOF!
YAWN!
ZZZZ!
I WAS JUST HAVING SOME LEFTOVERS, GRAB A PLATE!
THANKS, NOT NOW! HAVE YOU SEEN DENNIS?
NO. DO YOU NEED HELP LOOKING?
THE KIDS ARE MISSING!

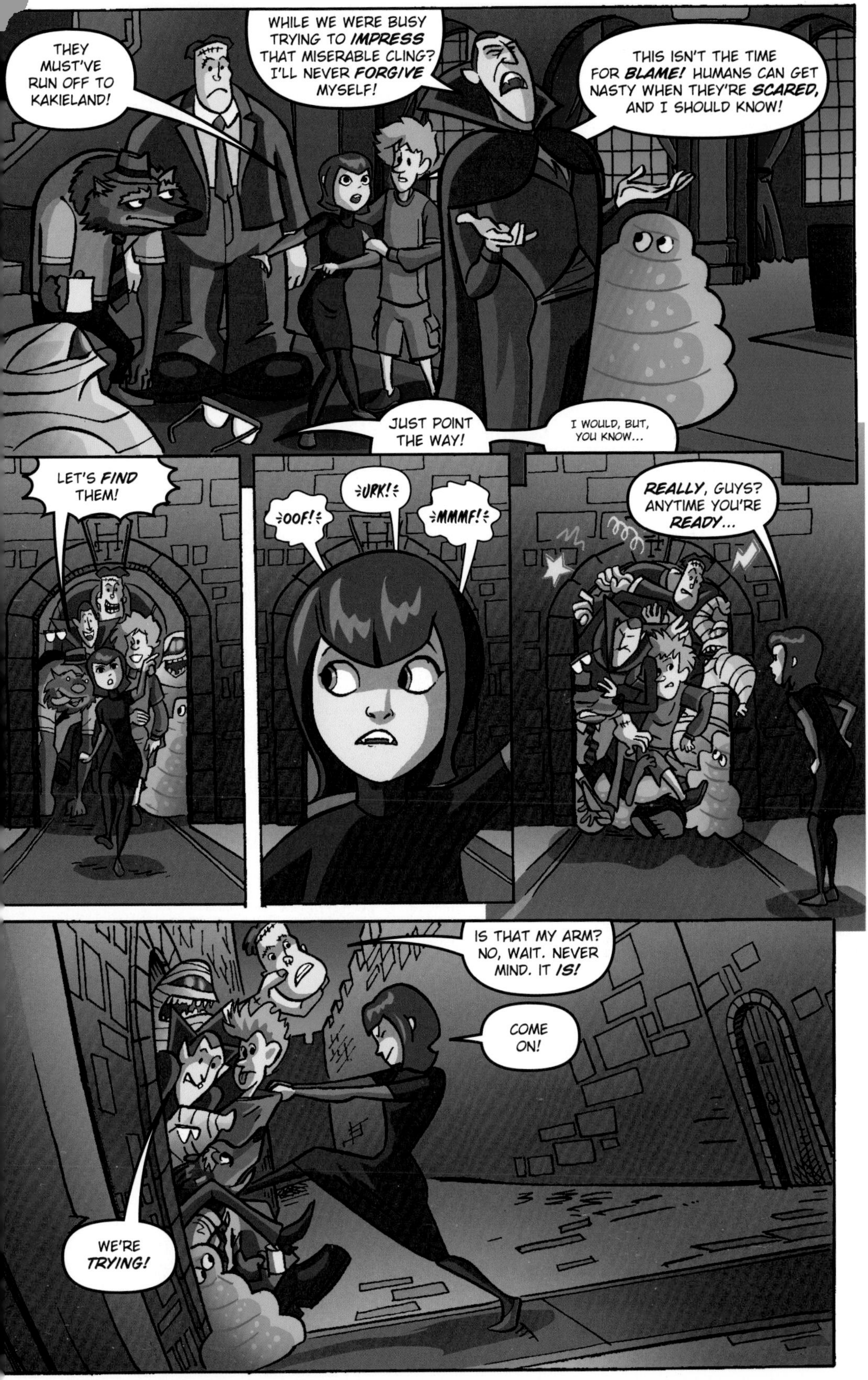
THEY MUST'VE RUN OFF TO KAKIELAND!
WHILE WE WERE BUSY TRYING TO IMPRESS THAT MISERABLE CLING? I'LL NEVER FORGIVE MYSELF!
THIS ISN'T THE TIME FOR BLAME! HUMANS CAN GET NASTY WHEN THEY'RE SCARED, AND I SHOULD KNOW!
JUST POINT THE WAY!
I WOULD, BUT, YOU KNOW...
LET'S FIND THEM!
OOF!
URK!
MMMF!
REALLY, GUYS? ANYTIME YOU'RE READY...
IS THAT MY ARM? NO, WAIT. NEVER MIND. IT IS!
COME ON!
WE'RE TRYING!

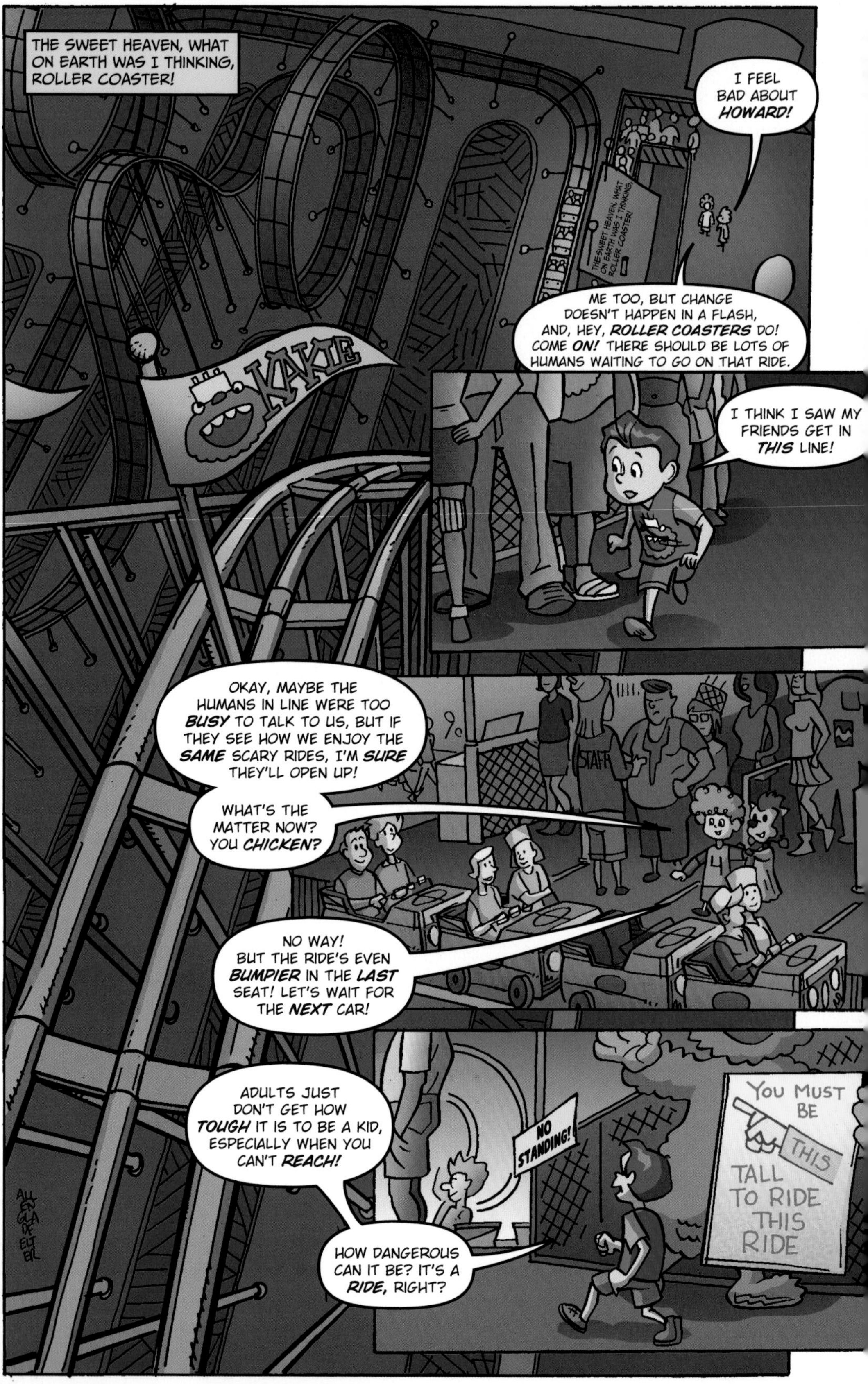
THE SWEET HEAVEN, WHAT ON EARTH WAS I THINKING, ROLLER COASTER!
I FEEL BAD ABOUT HOWARD!
ME TOO, BUT CHANGE DOESN'T HAPPEN IN A FLASH, AND, HEY, ROLLER COASTERS DO! COME ON! THERE SHOULD BE LOTS OF HUMANS WAITING TO GO ON THAT RIDE.
KAKIE
I THINK I SAW MY FRIENDS GET IN THIS LINE!
OKAY, MAYBE THE HUMANS IN LINE WERE TOO BUSY TO TALK TO US, BUT IF THEY SEE HOW WE ENJOY THE SAME SCARY RIDES, I'M SURE THEY'LL OPEN UP!
STAFF
WHAT'S THE MATTER NOW? YOU CHICKEN?
NO WAY! BUT THE RIDE'S EVEN BUMPIER IN THE LAST SEAT! LET'S WAIT FOR THE NEXT CAR!
ADULTS JUST DON'T GET HOW TOUGH IT IS TO BE A KID, ESPECIALLY WHEN YOU CAN'T REACH!
NO STANDING!
YOU MUST BE THIS TALL TO RIDE THIS RIDE
HOW DANGEROUS CAN IT BE? IT'S A RIDE, RIGHT?

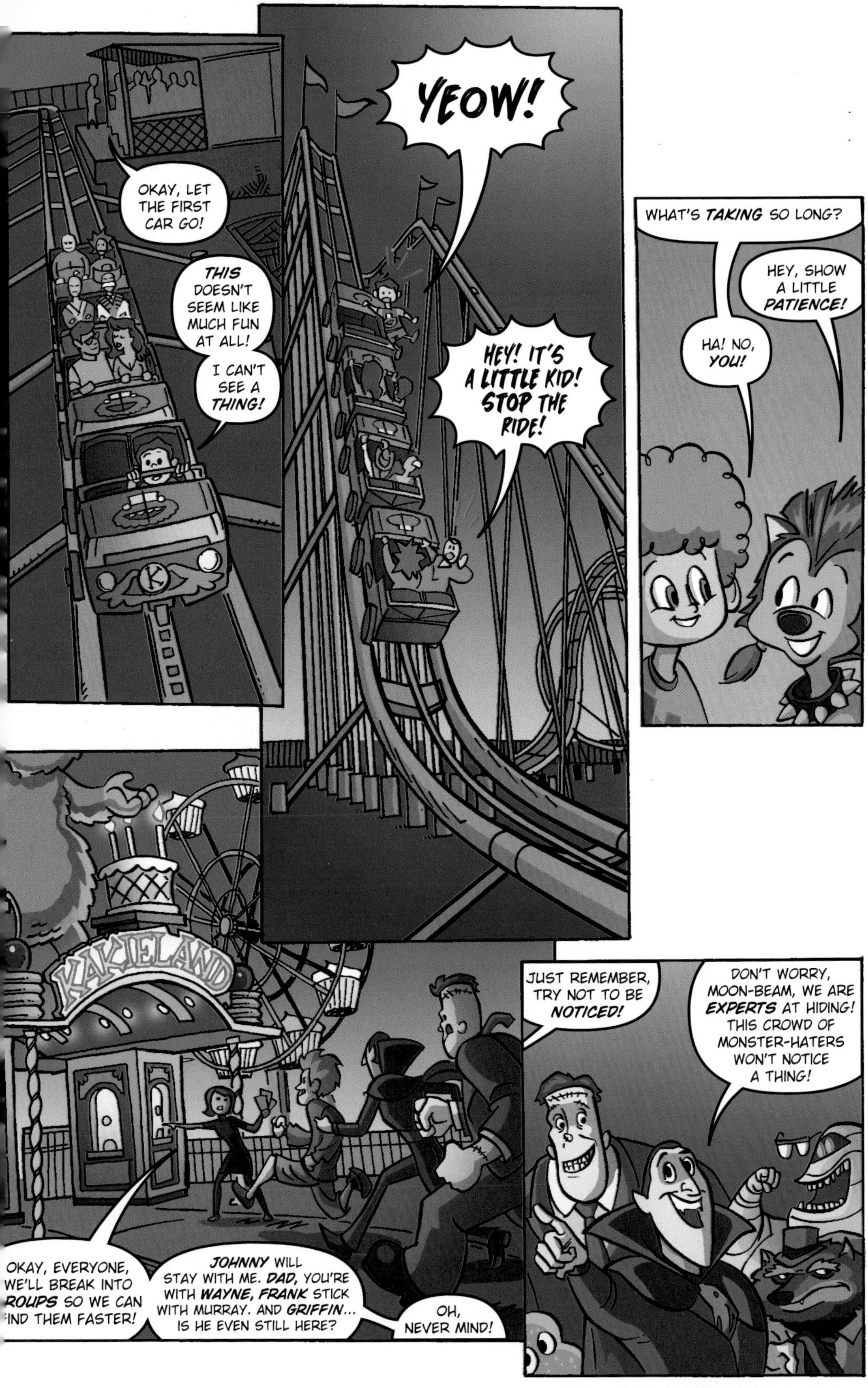
OKAY, LET THE FIRST CAR GO!
THIS DOESN'T SEEM LIKE MUCH FUN AT ALL!
I CAN'T SEE A THING!
YEOW!
HEY! IT'S A LITTLE KID! STOP THE RIDE!
WHAT'S TAKING SO LONG?
HEY, SHOW A LITTLE PATIENCE!
HA! NO, YOU!
KAKIELAND
OKAY, EVERYONE, WE'LL BREAK INTO ROUPS SO WE CAN FIND THEM FASTER!
JOHNNY WILL STAY WITH ME. DAD, YOU'RE WITH WAYNE, FRANK STICK WITH MURRAY. AND GRIFFIN... IS HE EVEN STILL HERE?
OH, NEVER MIND!
JUST REMEMBER, TRY NOT TO BE NOTICED!
DON'T WORRY, MOON-BEAM, WE ARE EXPERTS AT HIDING! THIS CROWD OF MONSTER-HATERS WON'T NOTICE A THING!

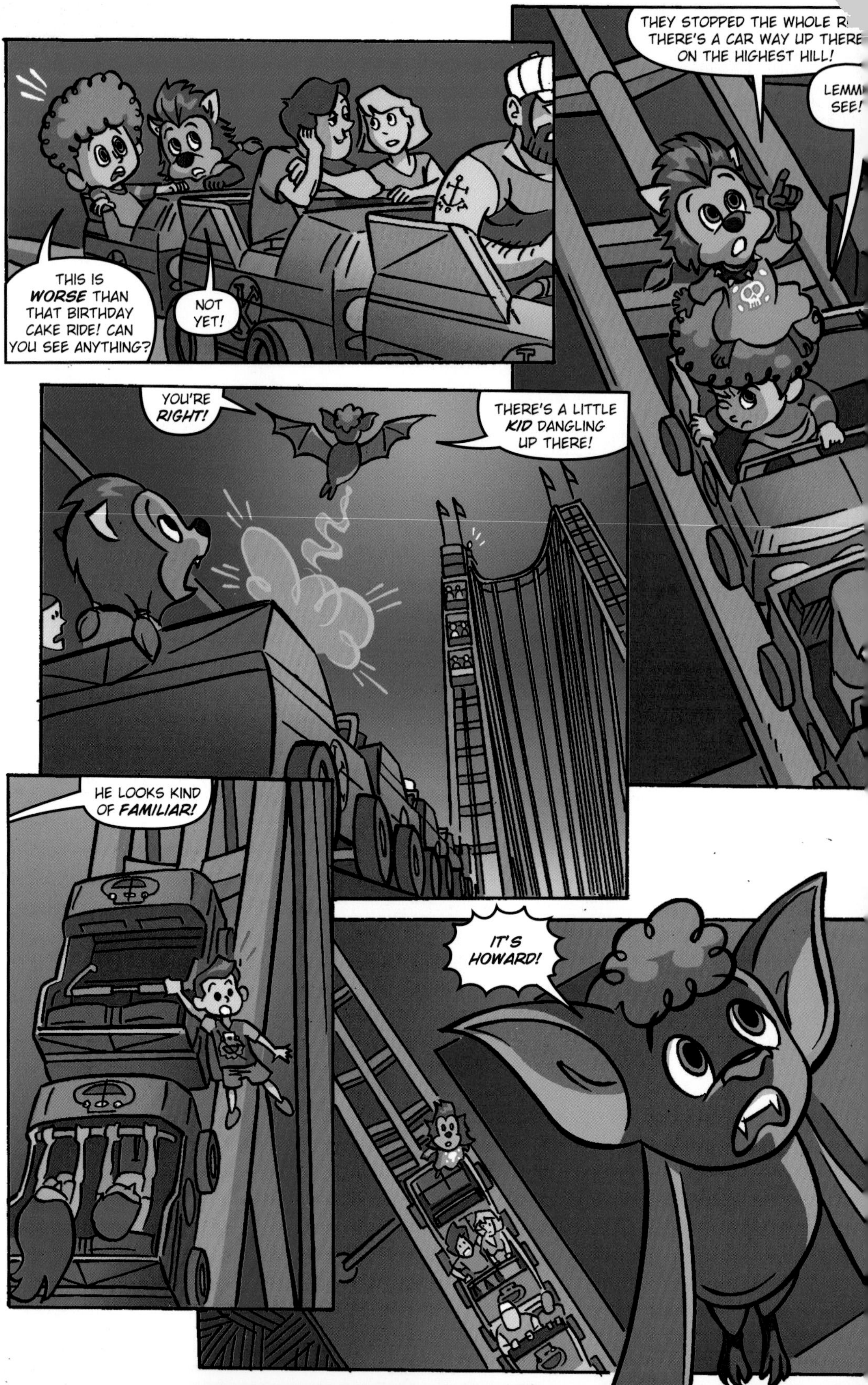
THIS IS *WORSE* THAN THAT BIRTHDAY CAKE RIDE! CAN YOU SEE ANYTHING?
NOT YET!
THEY STOPPED THE WHOLE R
THERE'S A CAR WAY UP THERE ON THE HIGHEST HILL!
LEMM SEE!
YOU'RE *RIGHT!*
THERE'S A LITTLE *KID* DANGLING UP THERE!
HE LOOKS KIND OF *FAMILIAR!*
IT'S HOWARD!

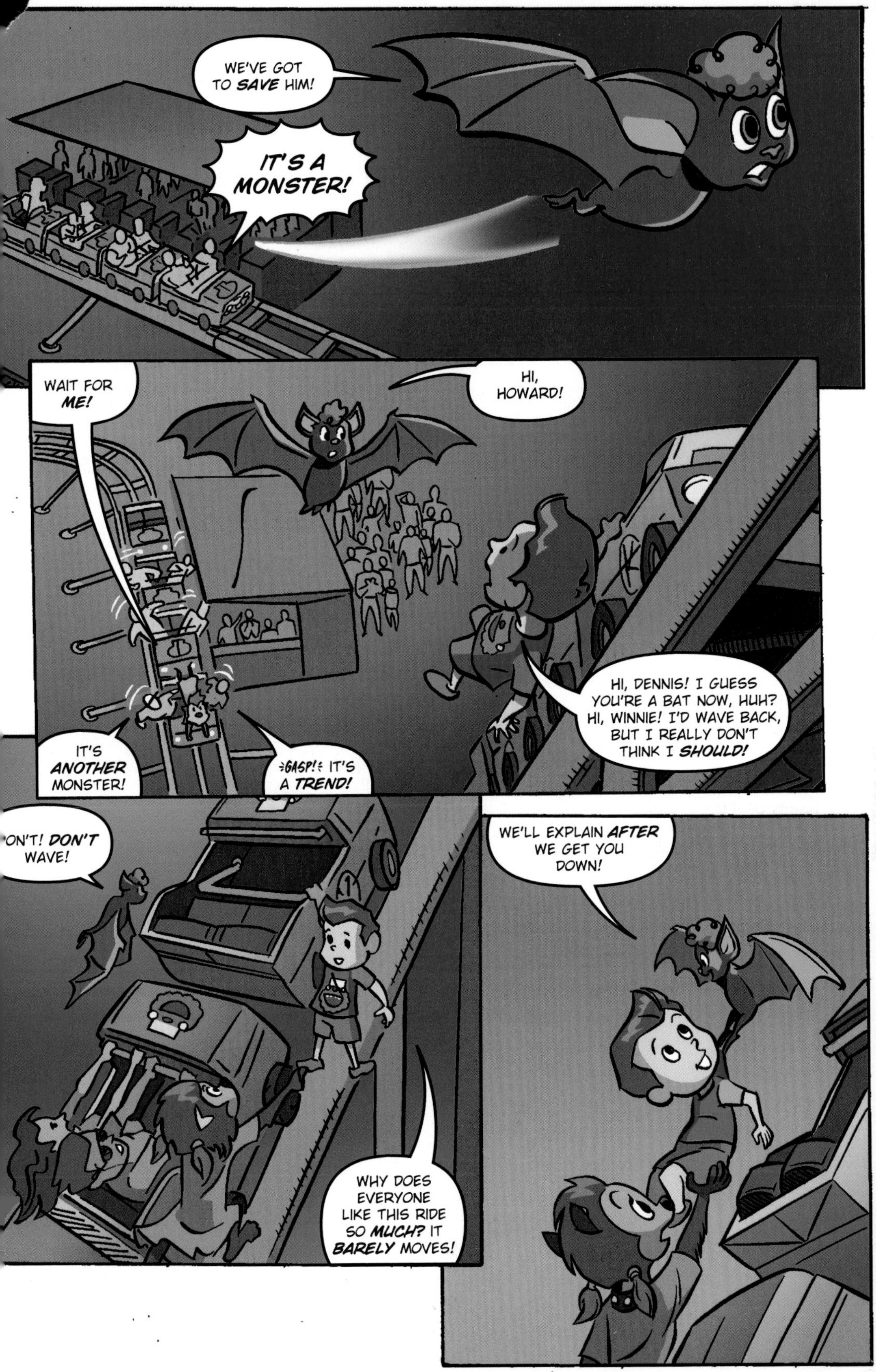
WE'VE GOT TO SAVE HIM!
IT'S A MONSTER!
WAIT FOR ME!
HI, HOWARD!
HI, DENNIS! I GUESS YOU'RE A BAT NOW, HUH? HI, WINNIE! I'D WAVE BACK, BUT I REALLY DON'T THINK I SHOULD!
IT'S ANOTHER MONSTER!
GASP! IT'S A TREND!
ON'T! DON'T WAVE!
WHY DOES EVERYONE LIKE THIS RIDE SO MUCH? IT BARELY MOVES!
WE'LL EXPLAIN AFTER WE GET YOU DOWN!

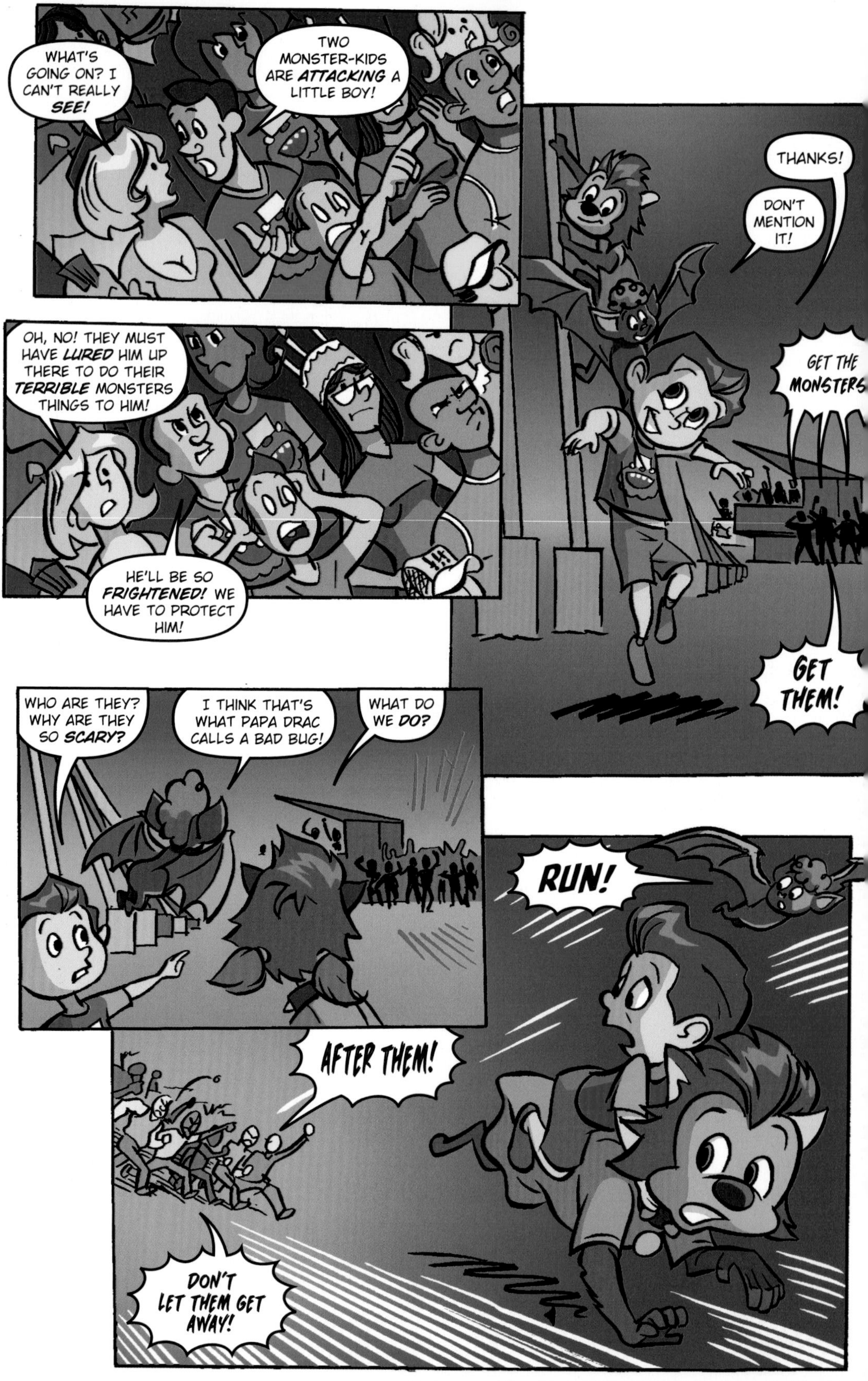
WHAT'S GOING ON? I CAN'T REALLY SEE!
TWO MONSTER-KIDS ARE ATTACKING A LITTLE BOY!
THANKS!
DON'T MENTION IT!
OH, NO! THEY MUST HAVE LURED HIM UP THERE TO DO THEIR TERRIBLE MONSTERS THINGS TO HIM!
HE'LL BE SO FRIGHTENED! WE HAVE TO PROTECT HIM!
GET THE MONSTERS
GET THEM!
WHO ARE THEY? WHY ARE THEY SO SCARY?
I THINK THAT'S WHAT PAPA DRAC CALLS A BAD BUG!
WHAT DO WE DO?
RUN!
AFTER THEM!
DON'T LET THEM GET AWAY!

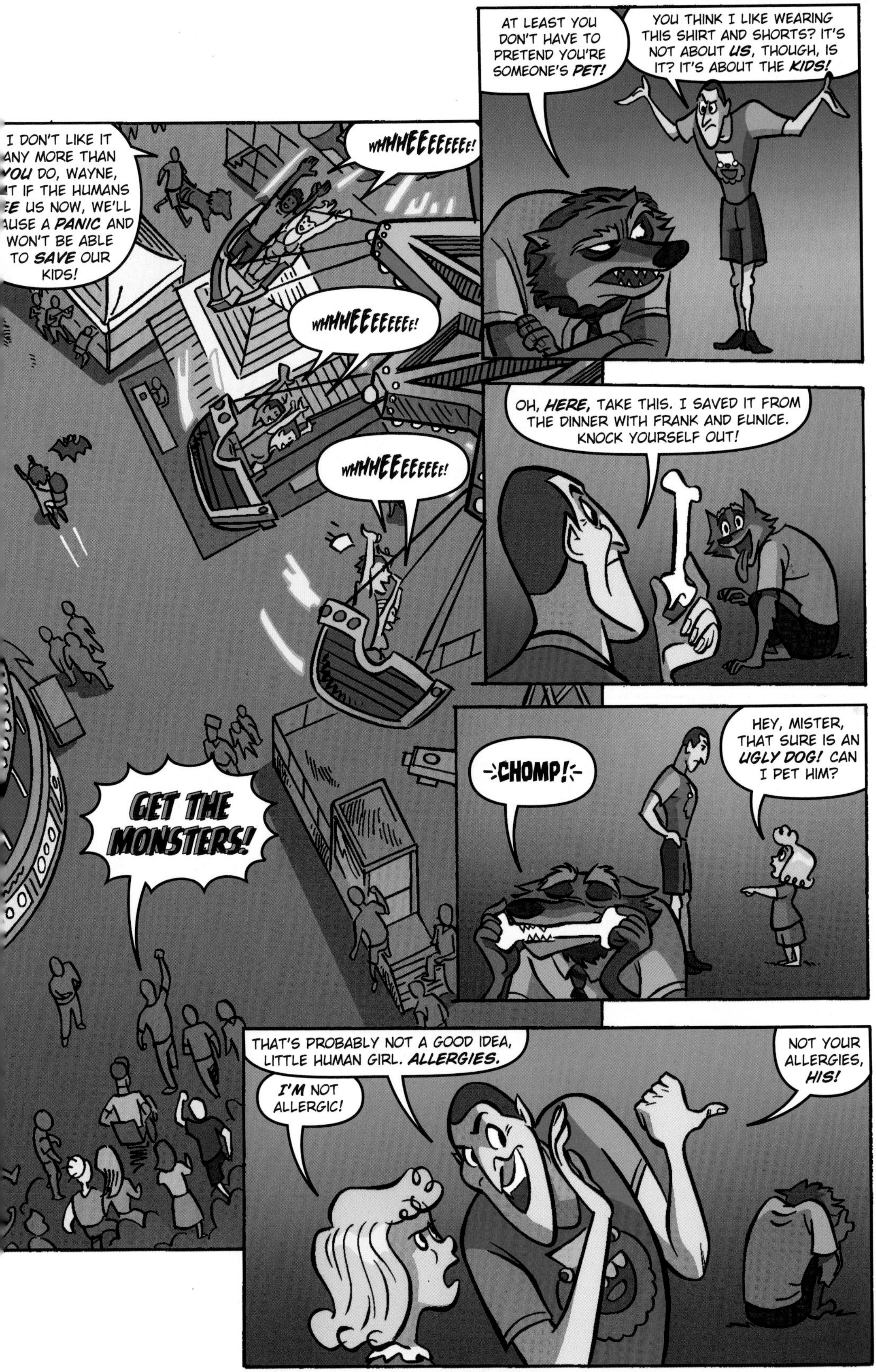
AT LEAST YOU DON'T HAVE TO PRETEND YOU'RE SOMEONE'S *PET!*
YOU THINK I LIKE WEARING THIS SHIRT AND SHORTS? IT'S NOT ABOUT *US*, THOUGH, IS IT? IT'S ABOUT THE *KIDS!*
I DON'T LIKE IT ANY MORE THAN *YOU* DO, WAYNE, IT IF THE HUMANS E US NOW, WE'LL AUSE A *PANIC* AND WON'T BE ABLE TO *SAVE* OUR KIDS!
WHHHEEEEEEEE!
WHHHEEEEEEEE!
WHHHEEEEEEEE!
GET THE MONSTERS!
OH, *HERE,* TAKE THIS. I SAVED IT FROM THE DINNER WITH FRANK AND EUNICE. KNOCK YOURSELF OUT!
-CHOMP!-
HEY, MISTER, THAT SURE IS AN *UGLY DOG!* CAN I PET HIM?
THAT'S PROBABLY NOT A GOOD IDEA, LITTLE HUMAN GIRL. *ALLERGIES.*
I'M NOT ALLERGIC!
NOT YOUR ALLERGIES, *HIS!*

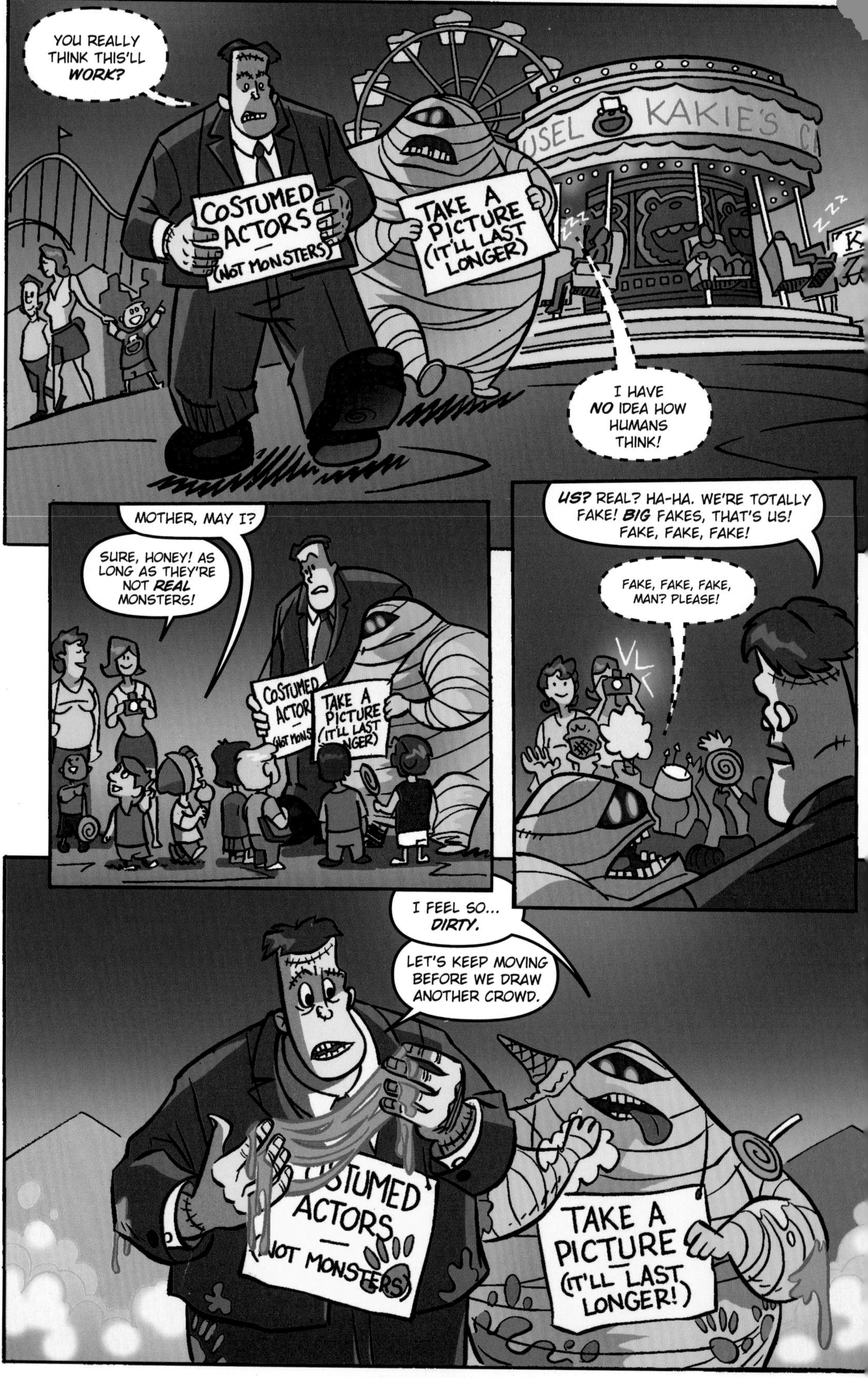
YOU REALLY THINK THIS'LL WORK?
COSTUMED ACTORS — (NOT MONSTERS)
TAKE A PICTURE (IT'LL LAST LONGER)
USEL KAKIE'S
I HAVE NO IDEA HOW HUMANS THINK!
MOTHER, MAY I?
SURE, HONEY! AS LONG AS THEY'RE NOT REAL MONSTERS!
US? REAL? HA-HA. WE'RE TOTALLY FAKE! BIG FAKES, THAT'S US! FAKE, FAKE, FAKE!
FAKE, FAKE, FAKE, MAN? PLEASE!
I FEEL SO... DIRTY.
LET'S KEEP MOVING BEFORE WE DRAW ANOTHER CROWD.
COSTUMED ACTORS — (NOT MONSTERS)
TAKE A PICTURE (IT'LL LAST LONGER!)

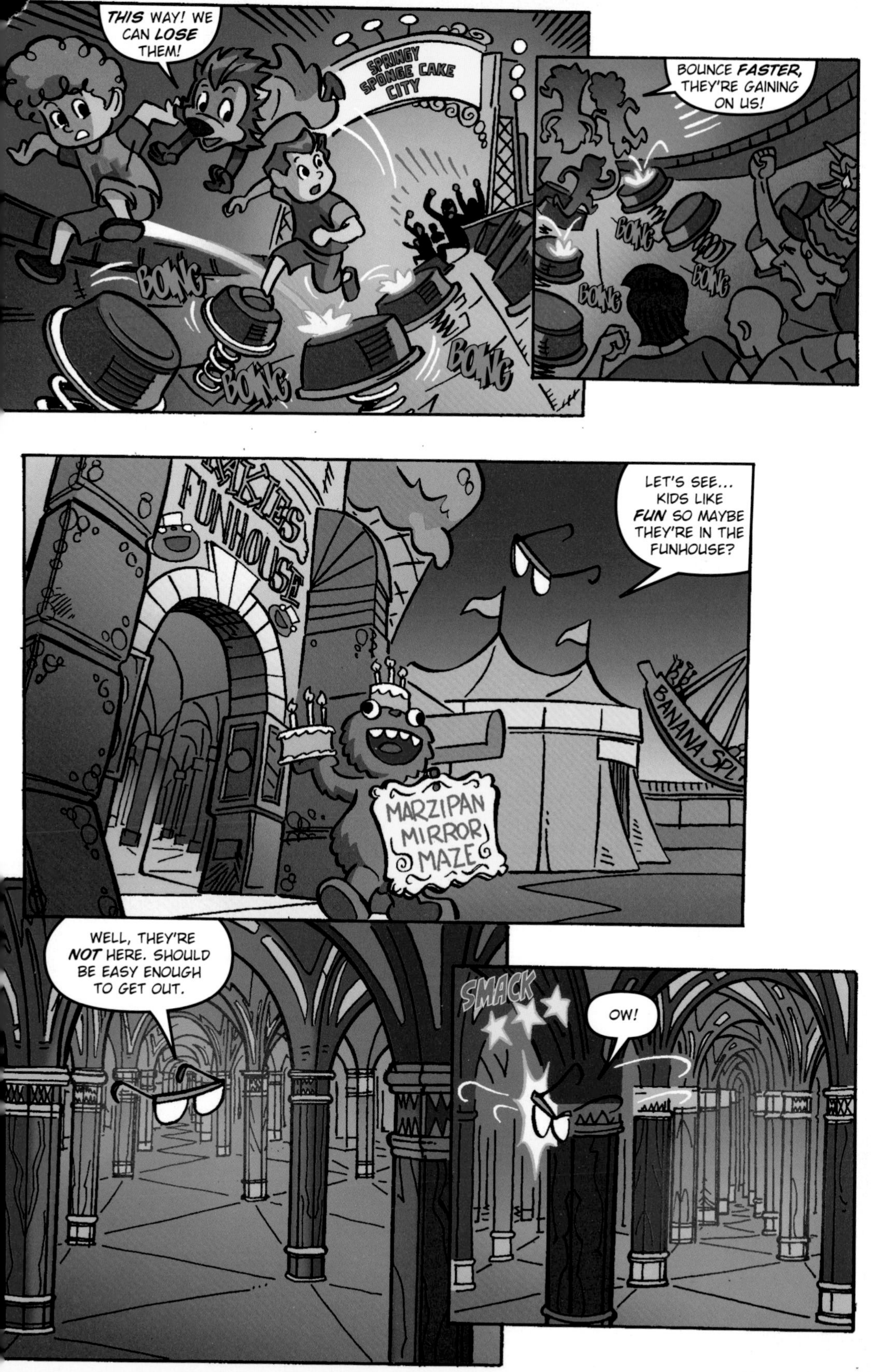
THIS WAY! WE CAN LOSE THEM!
SPRINGY SPONGE CAKE CITY
BOING
BOING
BOING
BOUNCE FASTER, THEY'RE GAINING ON US!
BOING
BOING
BOING
FUNHOUSE
LET'S SEE... KIDS LIKE FUN SO MAYBE THEY'RE IN THE FUNHOUSE?
MARZIPAN MIRROR MAZE
WELL, THEY'RE NOT HERE. SHOULD BE EASY ENOUGH TO GET OUT.
SMACK
OW!

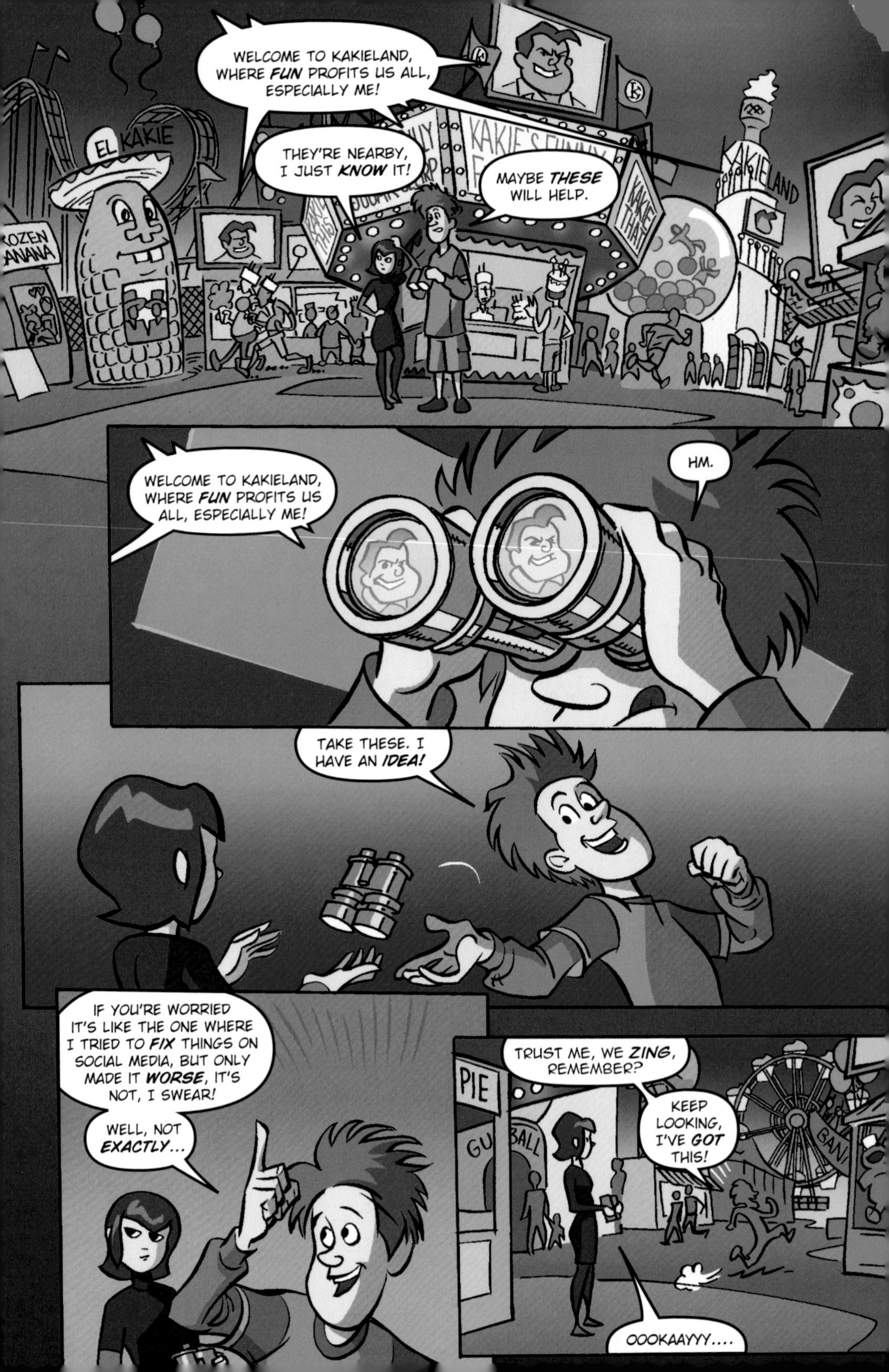
WELCOME TO KAKIELAND, WHERE FUN PROFITS US ALL, ESPECIALLY ME!
THEY'RE NEARBY, I JUST KNOW IT!
MAYBE THESE WILL HELP.
EL KAKIE
KAKIELAND
WELCOME TO KAKIELAND, WHERE FUN PROFITS US ALL, ESPECIALLY ME!
HM.
TAKE THESE. I HAVE AN IDEA!
IF YOU'RE WORRIED IT'S LIKE THE ONE WHERE I TRIED TO FIX THINGS ON SOCIAL MEDIA, BUT ONLY MADE IT WORSE, IT'S NOT, I SWEAR!
WELL, NOT EXACTLY...
TRUST ME, WE ZING, REMEMBER?
KEEP LOOKING, I'VE GOT THIS!
PIE
OOOKAAYYY....

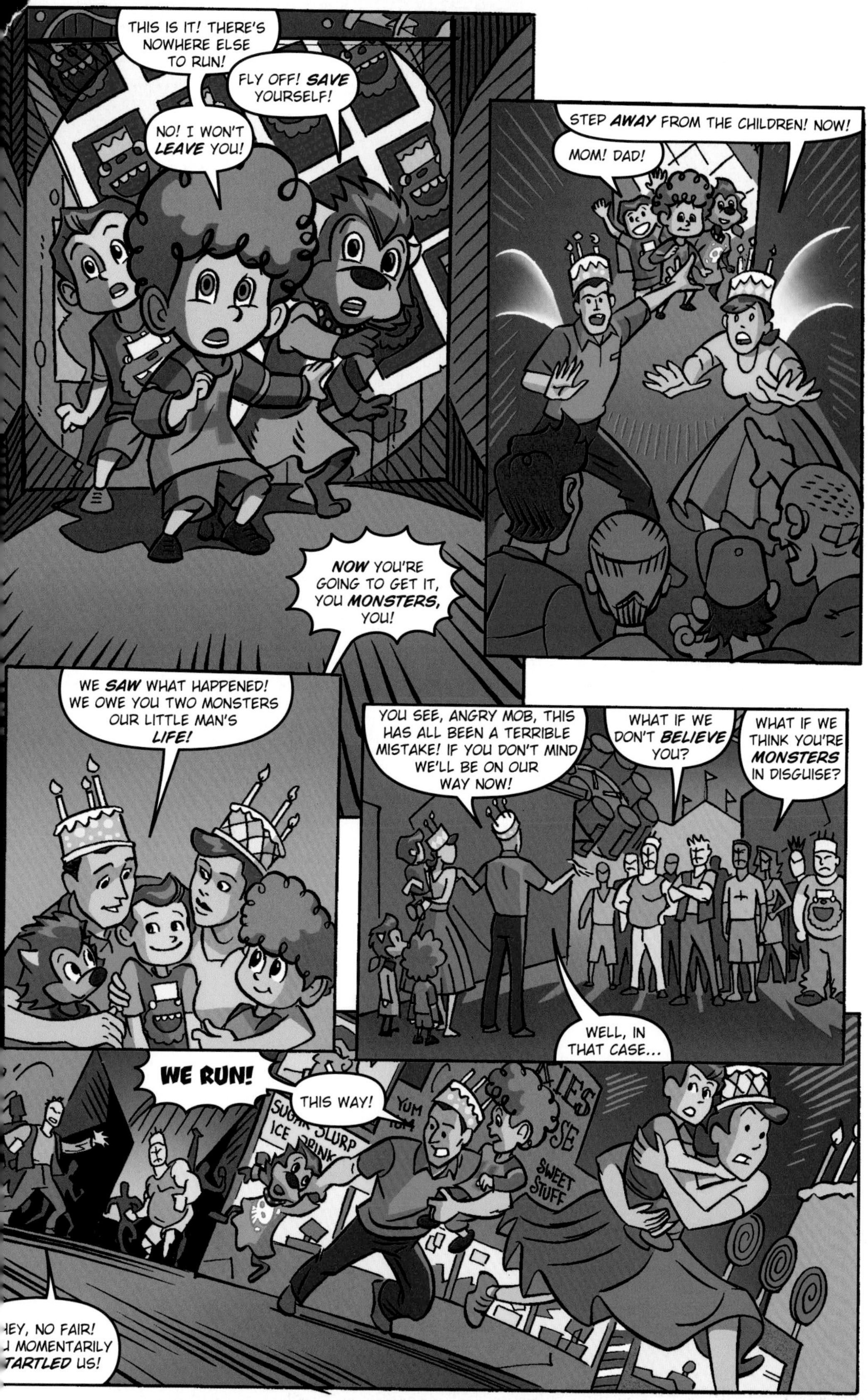
THIS IS IT! THERE'S NOWHERE ELSE TO RUN!
FLY OFF! SAVE YOURSELF!
NO! I WON'T LEAVE YOU!
STEP AWAY FROM THE CHILDREN! NOW!
MOM! DAD!
NOW YOU'RE GOING TO GET IT, YOU MONSTERS, YOU!
WE SAW WHAT HAPPENED! WE OWE YOU TWO MONSTERS OUR LITTLE MAN'S LIFE!
YOU SEE, ANGRY MOB, THIS HAS ALL BEEN A TERRIBLE MISTAKE! IF YOU DON'T MIND WE'LL BE ON OUR WAY NOW!
WHAT IF WE DON'T BELIEVE YOU?
WHAT IF WE THINK YOU'RE MONSTERS IN DISGUISE?
WELL, IN THAT CASE...
WE RUN!
THIS WAY!
SUGAR SLURP ICE DRINK
YUM
SWEET STUFF
HEY, NO FAIR!
MOMENTARILY
TARTLED US!

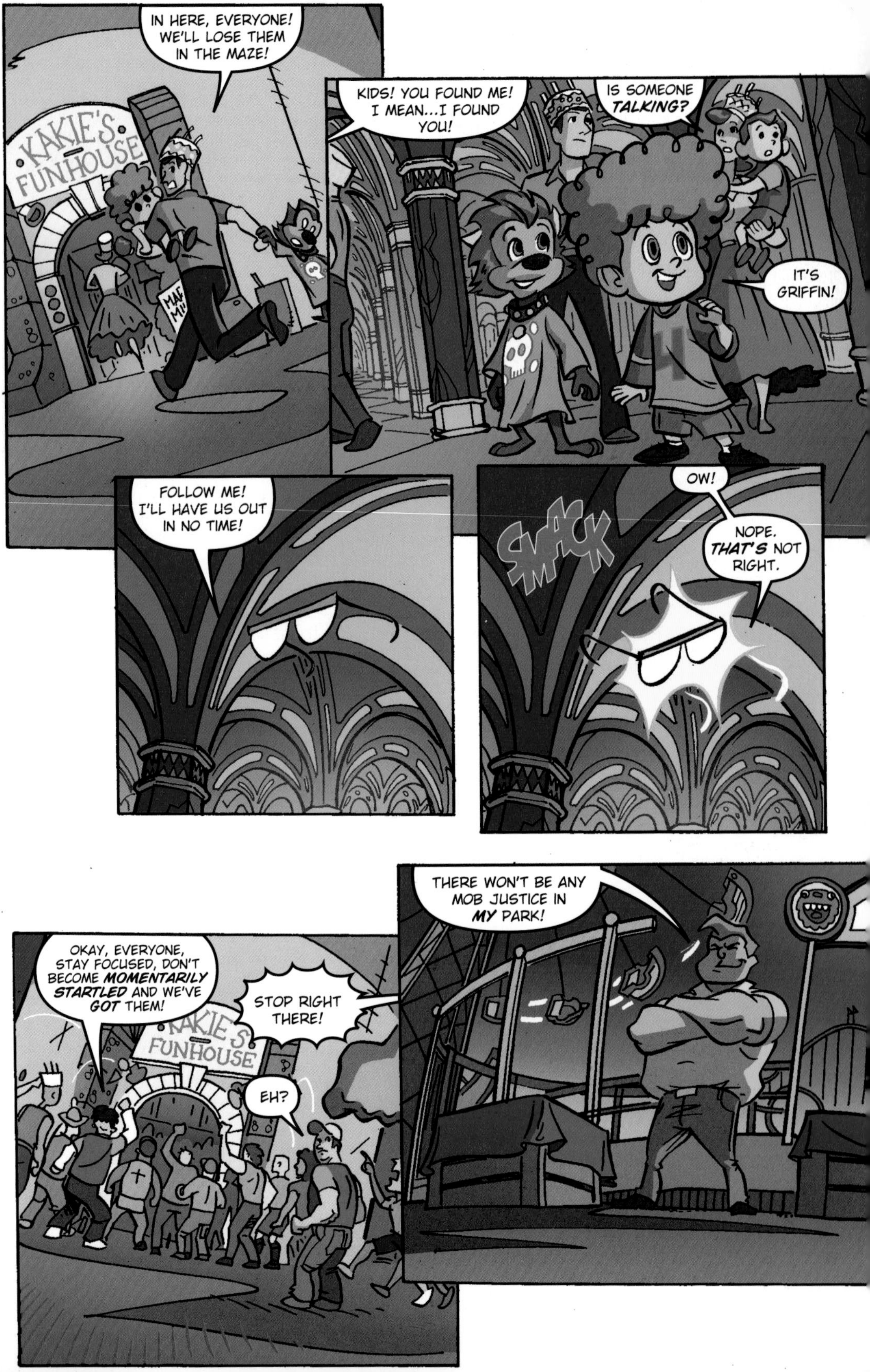
IN HERE, EVERYONE! WE'LL LOSE THEM IN THE MAZE!
KAKIE'S FUNHOUSE
KIDS! YOU FOUND ME! I MEAN...I FOUND YOU!
IS SOMEONE *TALKING?*
IT'S GRIFFIN!
FOLLOW ME! I'LL HAVE US OUT IN NO TIME!
SMACK
OW!
NOPE. ***THAT'S*** NOT RIGHT.
OKAY, EVERYONE, STAY FOCUSED, DON'T BECOME ***MOMENTARILY STARTLED*** AND WE'VE ***GOT*** THEM!
KAKIE'S FUNHOUSE
STOP RIGHT THERE!
EH?
THERE WON'T BE ANY MOB JUSTICE IN ***MY*** PARK!

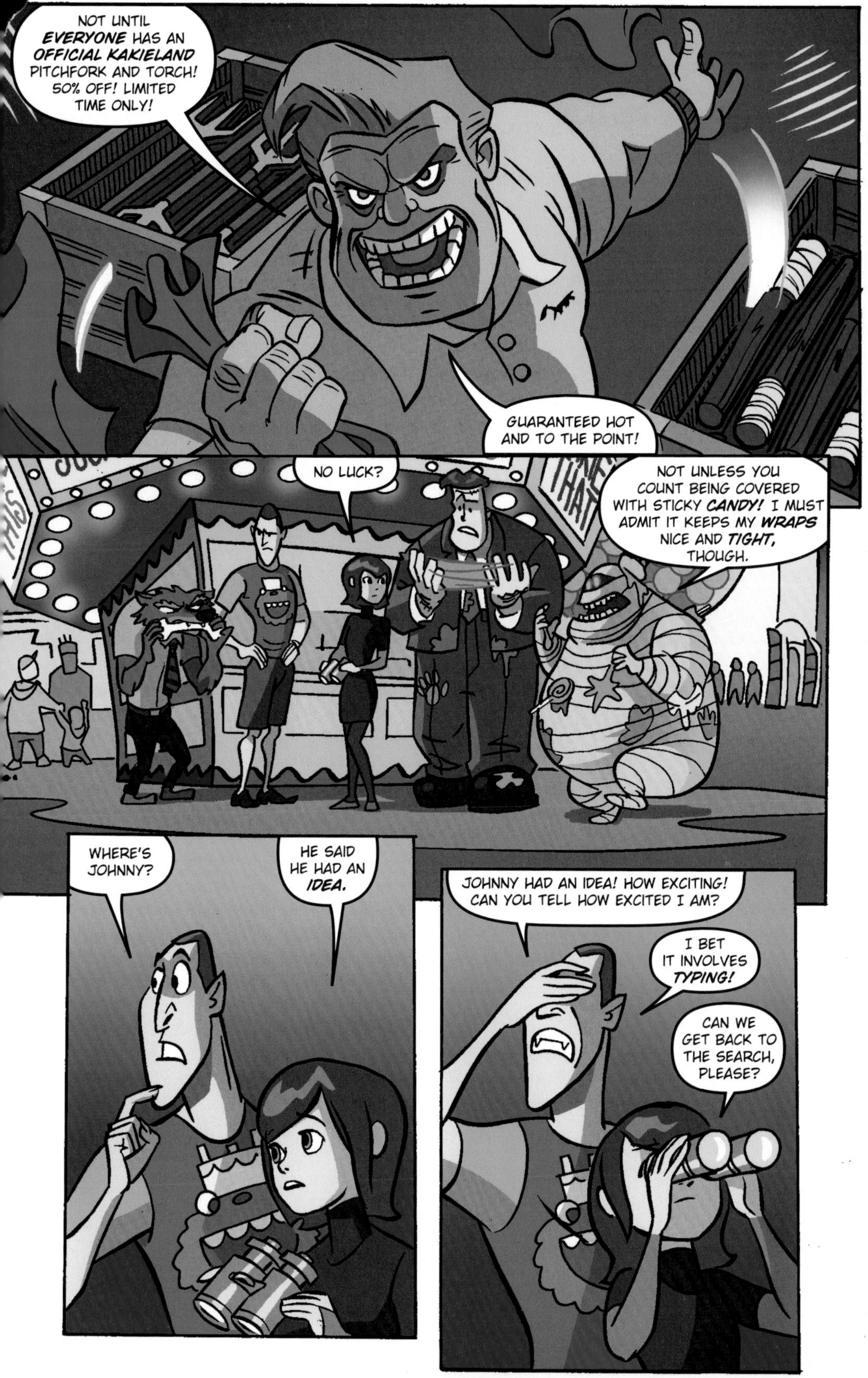
NOT UNTIL EVERYONE HAS AN OFFICIAL KAKIELAND PITCHFORK AND TORCH! 50% OFF! LIMITED TIME ONLY!
GUARANTEED HOT AND TO THE POINT!
NO LUCK?
NOT UNLESS YOU COUNT BEING COVERED WITH STICKY CANDY! I MUST ADMIT IT KEEPS MY WRAPS NICE AND TIGHT, THOUGH.
WHERE'S JOHNNY?
HE SAID HE HAD AN IDEA.
JOHNNY HAD AN IDEA! HOW EXCITING! CAN YOU TELL HOW EXCITED I AM?
I BET IT INVOLVES TYPING!
CAN WE GET BACK TO THE SEARCH, PLEASE?

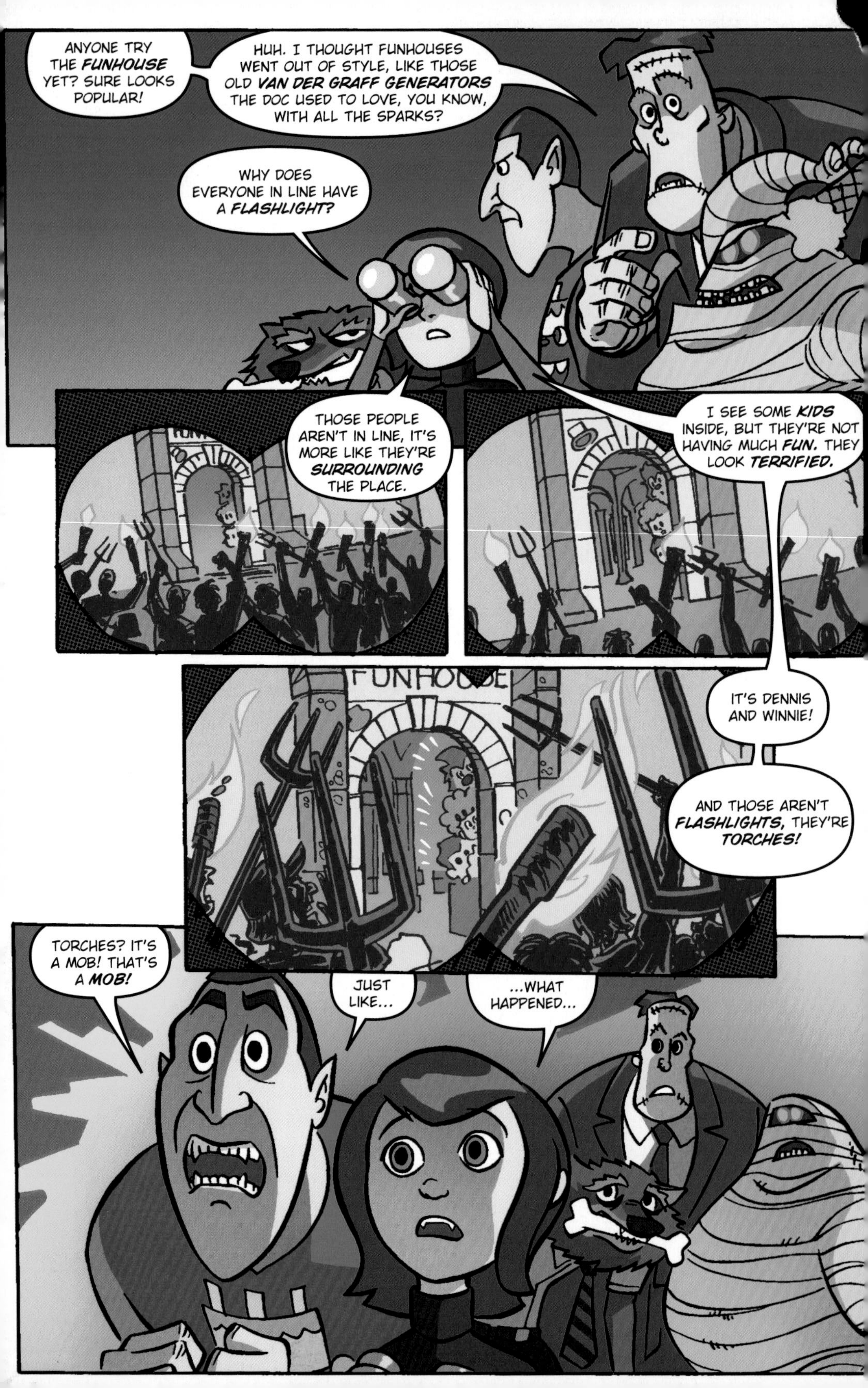

ANYONE TRY THE FUNHOUSE YET? SURE LOOKS POPULAR!
HUH. I THOUGHT FUNHOUSES WENT OUT OF STYLE, LIKE THOSE OLD VAN DER GRAFF GENERATORS THE DOC USED TO LOVE, YOU KNOW, WITH ALL THE SPARKS?
WHY DOES EVERYONE IN LINE HAVE A FLASHLIGHT?
THOSE PEOPLE AREN'T IN LINE, IT'S MORE LIKE THEY'RE SURROUNDING THE PLACE.
I SEE SOME KIDS INSIDE, BUT THEY'RE NOT HAVING MUCH FUN. THEY LOOK TERRIFIED.
FUNHOUSE
IT'S DENNIS AND WINNIE!
AND THOSE AREN'T FLASHLIGHTS, THEY'RE TORCHES!
TORCHES? IT'S A MOB! THAT'S A MOB!
JUST LIKE...
...WHAT HAPPENED...

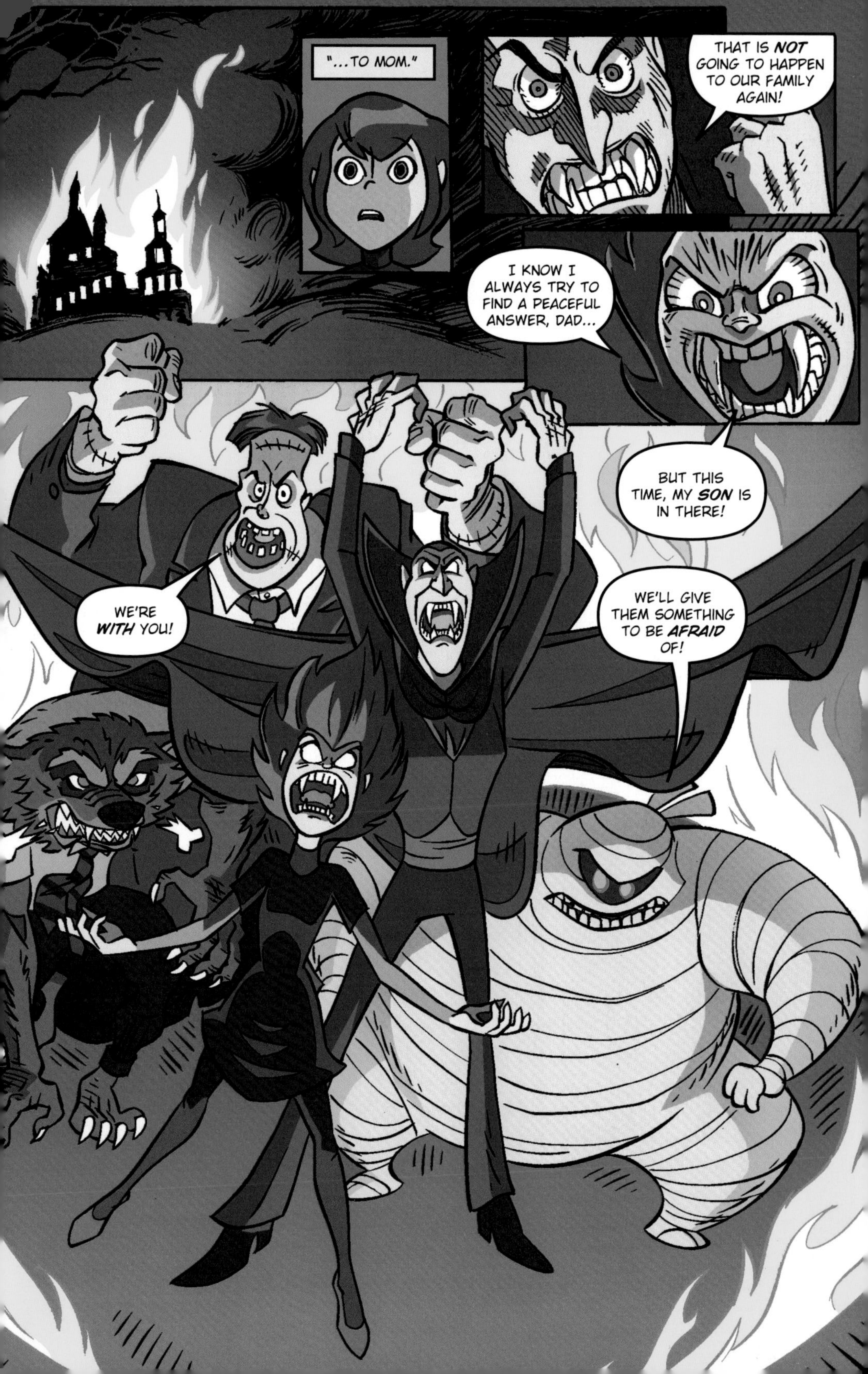
"...TO MOM."
THAT IS NOT GOING TO HAPPEN TO OUR FAMILY AGAIN!
I KNOW I ALWAYS TRY TO FIND A PEACEFUL ANSWER, DAD...
BUT THIS TIME, MY SON IS IN THERE!
WE'RE WITH YOU!
WE'LL GIVE THEM SOMETHING TO BE AFRAID OF!

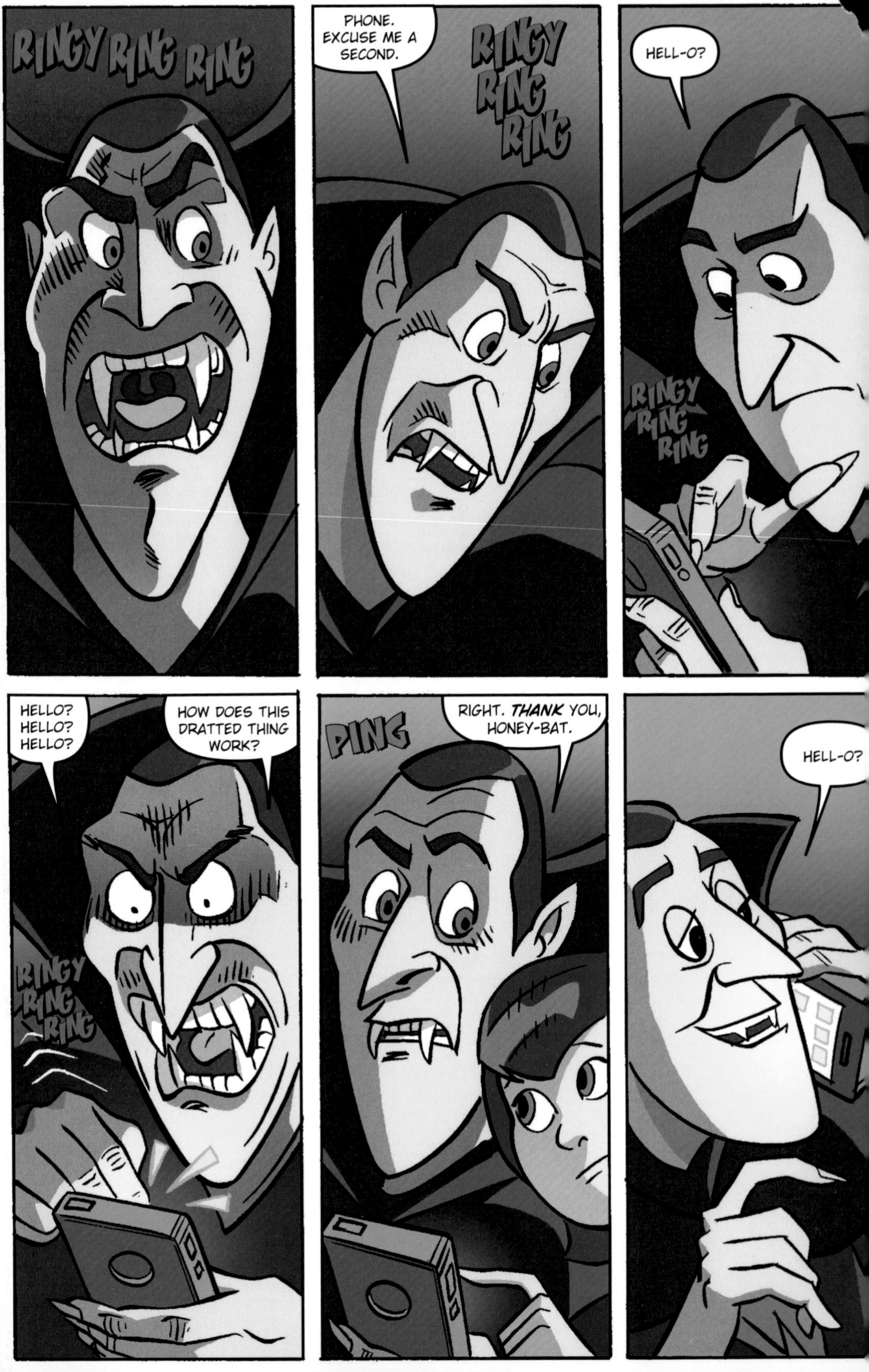
RINGY RING RING
PHONE. EXCUSE ME A SECOND.
RINGY RING RING
HELL-O?
RINGY RING RING
HELLO? HELLO? HELLO?
HOW DOES THIS DRATTED THING WORK?
RINGY RING RING
PING
RIGHT. THANK YOU, HONEY-BAT.
HELL-O?

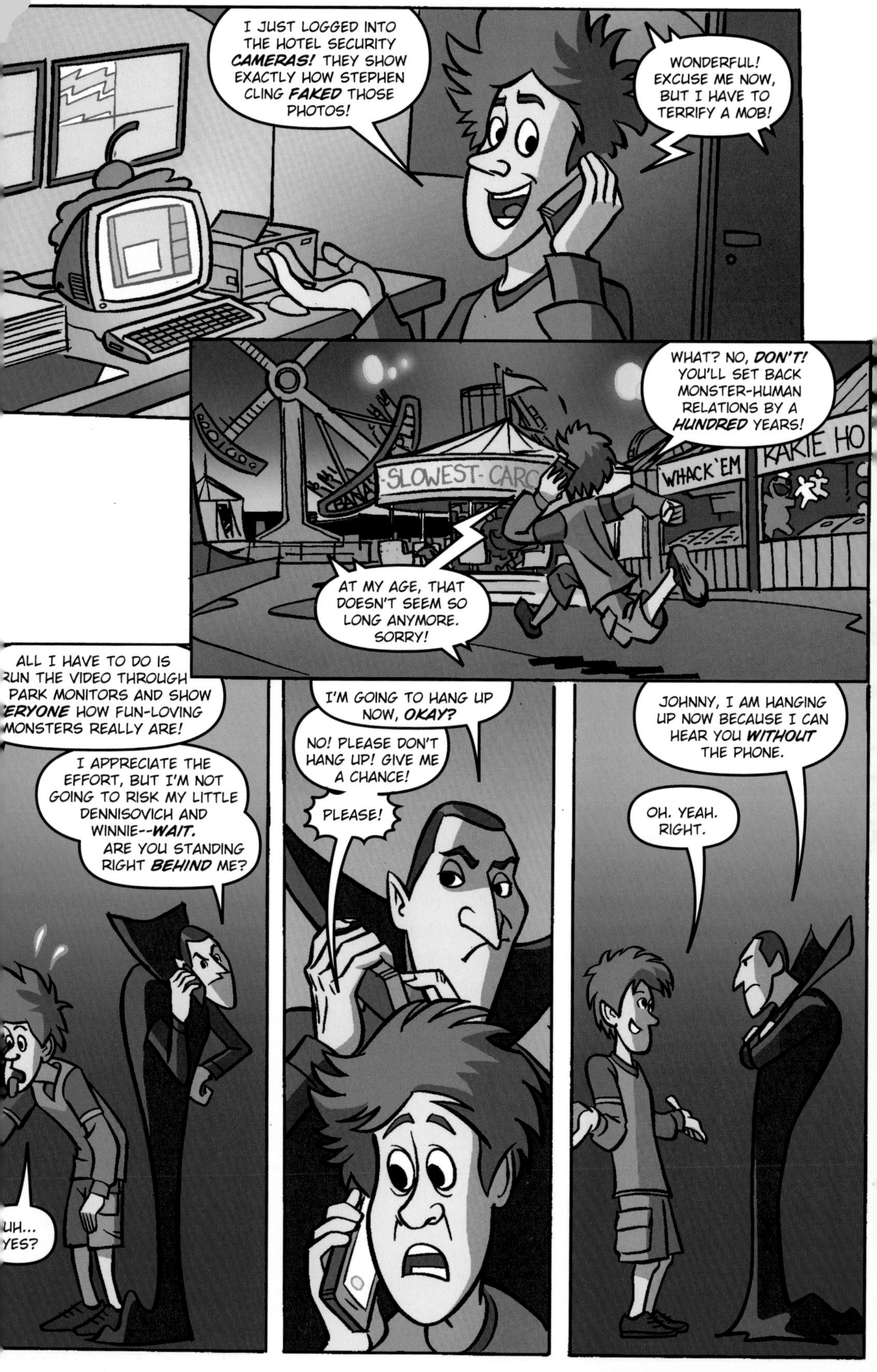
I JUST LOGGED INTO THE HOTEL SECURITY CAMERAS! THEY SHOW EXACTLY HOW STEPHEN CLING FAKED THOSE PHOTOS!
WONDERFUL! EXCUSE ME NOW, BUT I HAVE TO TERRIFY A MOB!
WHAT? NO, DON'T! YOU'LL SET BACK MONSTER-HUMAN RELATIONS BY A HUNDRED YEARS!
SLOWEST CARO
WHACK 'EM
KARIE HO
AT MY AGE, THAT DOESN'T SEEM SO LONG ANYMORE. SORRY!
ALL I HAVE TO DO IS RUN THE VIDEO THROUGH PARK MONITORS AND SHOW ERYONE HOW FUN-LOVING MONSTERS REALLY ARE!
I APPRECIATE THE EFFORT, BUT I'M NOT GOING TO RISK MY LITTLE DENNISOVICH AND WINNIE--WAIT. ARE YOU STANDING RIGHT BEHIND ME?
UH... YES?
I'M GOING TO HANG UP NOW, OKAY?
NO! PLEASE DON'T HANG UP! GIVE ME A CHANCE!
PLEASE!
JOHNNY, I AM HANGING UP NOW BECAUSE I CAN HEAR YOU WITHOUT THE PHONE.
OH. YEAH. RIGHT.

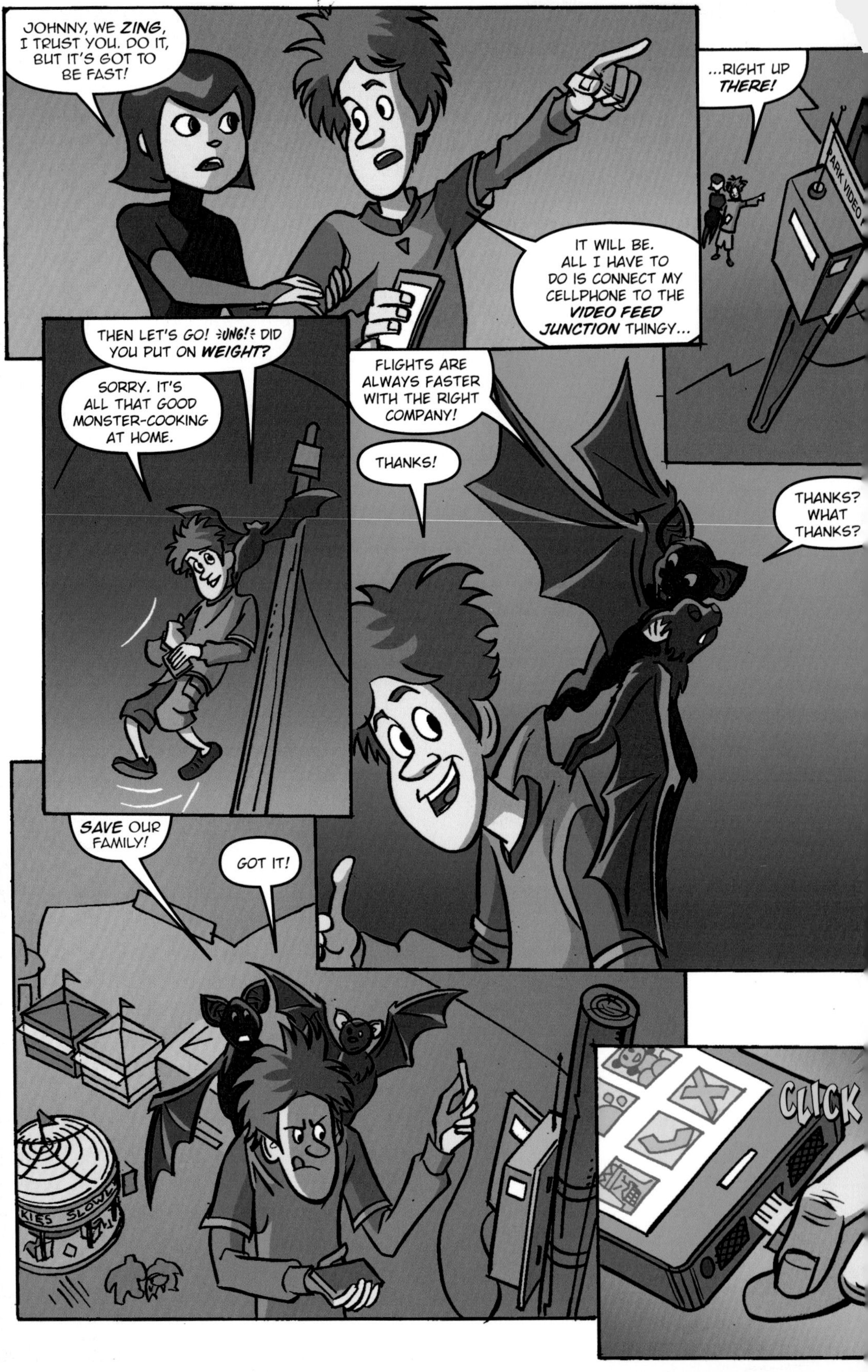

JOHNNY, WE *ZING*, I TRUST YOU. DO IT, BUT IT'S GOT TO BE FAST!
IT WILL BE. ALL I HAVE TO DO IS CONNECT MY CELLPHONE TO THE ***VIDEO FEED JUNCTION*** THINGY...
...RIGHT UP ***THERE!***
PARK VIDEO
THEN LET'S GO! UNG! DID YOU PUT ON ***WEIGHT?***
SORRY. IT'S ALL THAT GOOD MONSTER-COOKING AT HOME.
FLIGHTS ARE ALWAYS FASTER WITH THE RIGHT COMPANY!
THANKS!
THANKS? WHAT THANKS?
SAVE OUR FAMILY!
GOT IT!
KIES SLOW
CLICK

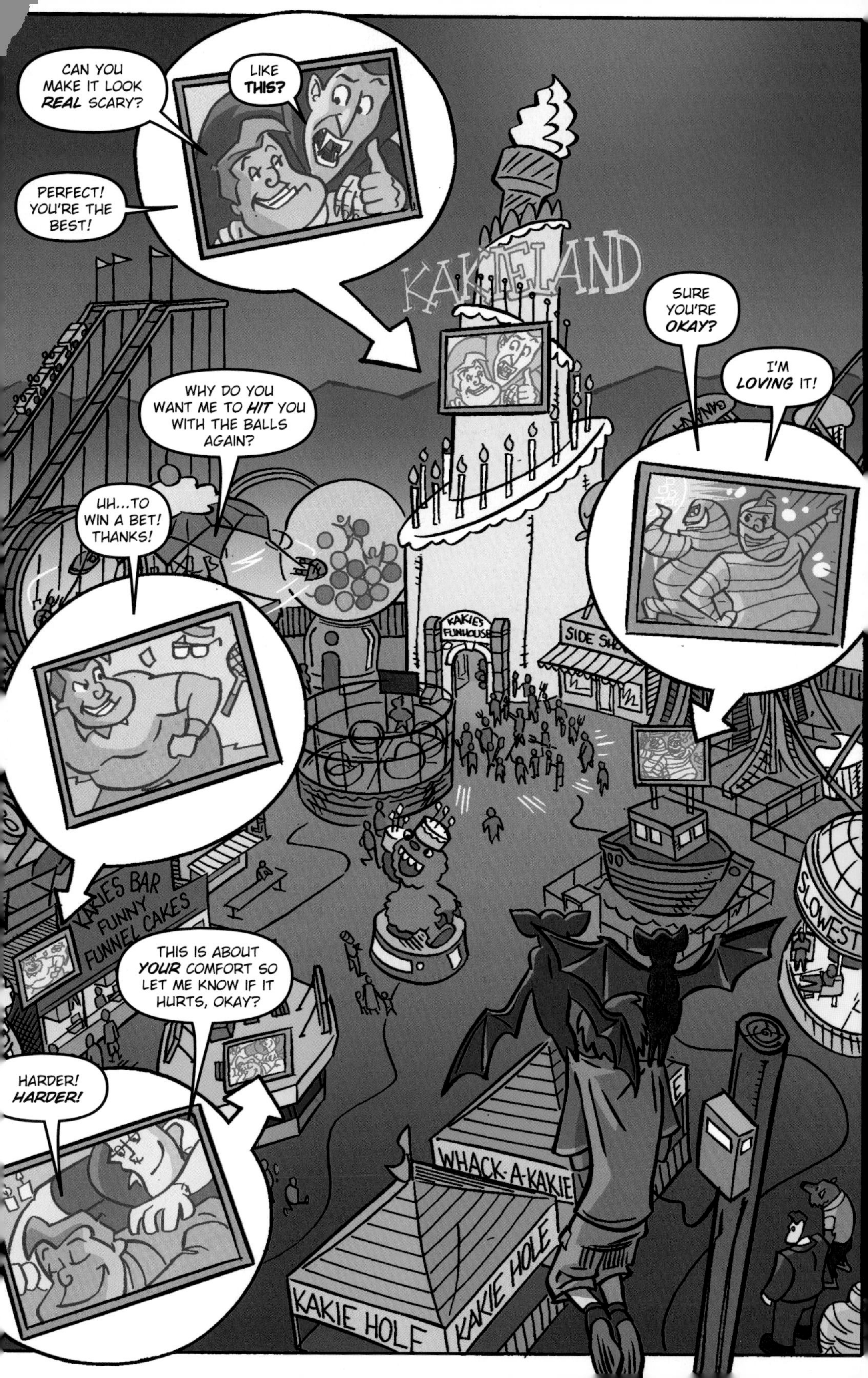
CAN YOU MAKE IT LOOK REAL SCARY?
LIKE THIS?
PERFECT! YOU'RE THE BEST!
KAKIELAND
SURE YOU'RE OKAY?
I'M LOVING IT!
WHY DO YOU WANT ME TO HIT YOU WITH THE BALLS AGAIN?
UH...TO WIN A BET! THANKS!
KAKIES FUNHOUSE
SIDE SHOW
KAKIES BAR FUNNY FUNNEL CAKES
SLOWEST
THIS IS ABOUT YOUR COMFORT SO LET ME KNOW IF IT HURTS, OKAY?
HARDER! HARDER!
WHACK-A-KAKIE
KAKIE HOLE
KAKIE HOLE

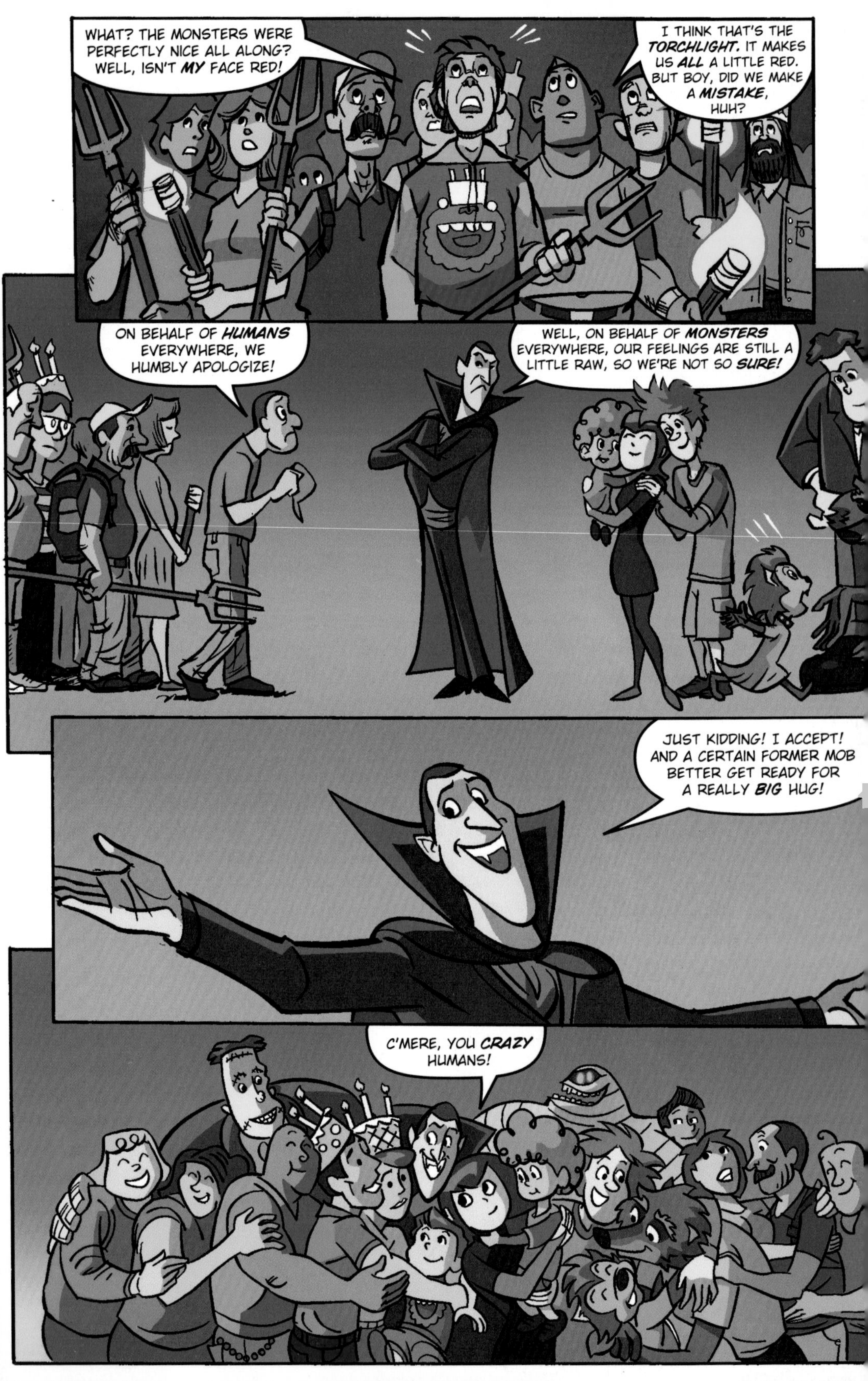
WHAT? THE MONSTERS WERE PERFECTLY NICE ALL ALONG? WELL, ISN'T MY FACE RED!
I THINK THAT'S THE TORCHLIGHT. IT MAKES US ALL A LITTLE RED. BUT BOY, DID WE MAKE A MISTAKE, HUH?
ON BEHALF OF HUMANS EVERYWHERE, WE HUMBLY APOLOGIZE!
WELL, ON BEHALF OF MONSTERS EVERYWHERE, OUR FEELINGS ARE STILL A LITTLE RAW, SO WE'RE NOT SO SURE!
JUST KIDDING! I ACCEPT! AND A CERTAIN FORMER MOB BETTER GET READY FOR A REALLY BIG HUG!
C'MERE, YOU CRAZY HUMANS!

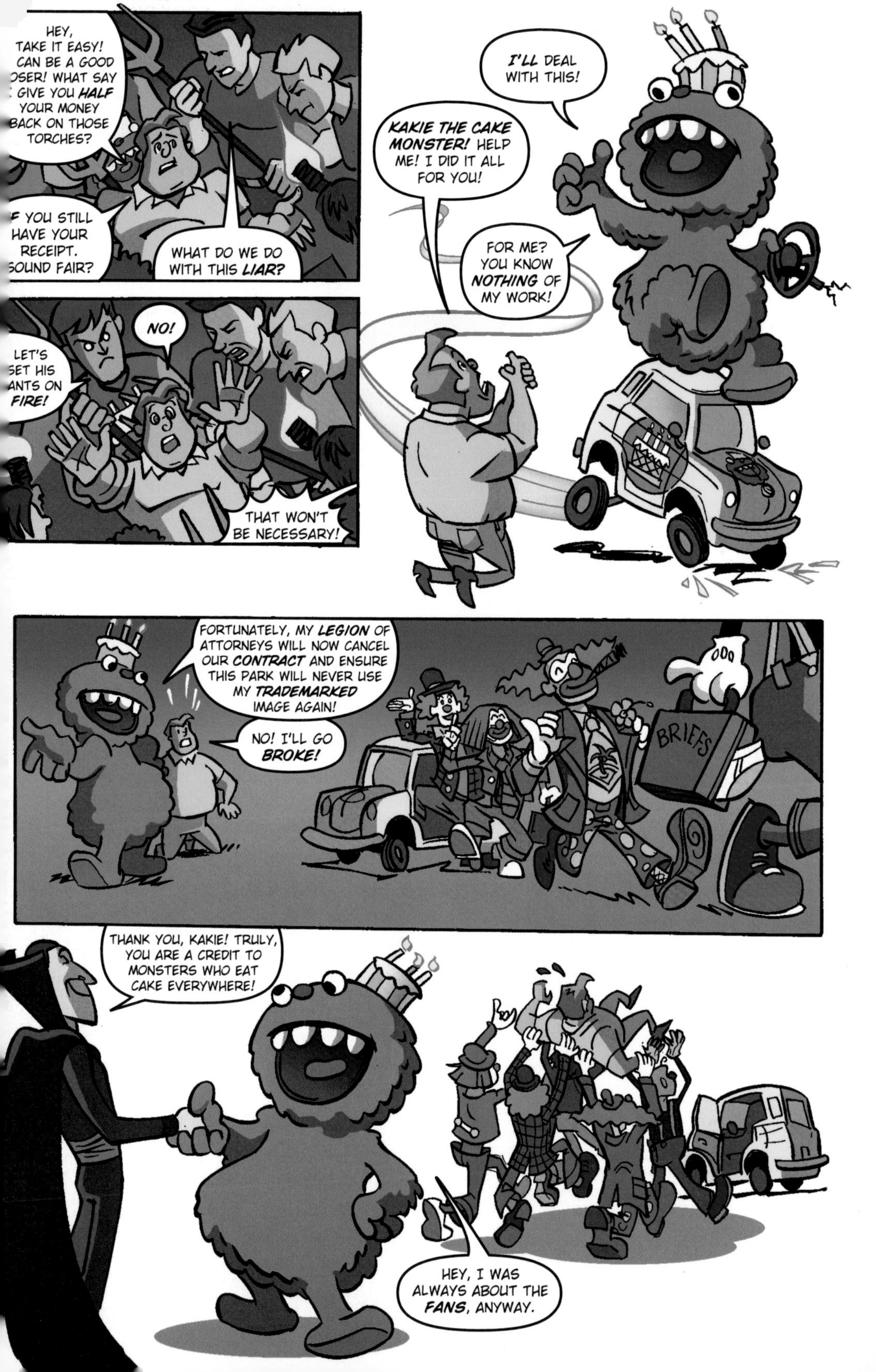
HEY, TAKE IT EASY! CAN BE A GOOD OSER! WHAT SAY GIVE YOU HALF YOUR MONEY BACK ON THOSE TORCHES?
F YOU STILL HAVE YOUR RECEIPT. SOUND FAIR?
WHAT DO WE DO WITH THIS LIAR?
LET'S SET HIS ANTS ON FIRE!
NO!
THAT WON'T BE NECESSARY!
I'LL DEAL WITH THIS!
KAKIE THE CAKE MONSTER! HELP ME! I DID IT ALL FOR YOU!
FOR ME? YOU KNOW NOTHING OF MY WORK!
FORTUNATELY, MY LEGION OF ATTORNEYS WILL NOW CANCEL OUR CONTRACT AND ENSURE THIS PARK WILL NEVER USE MY TRADEMARKED IMAGE AGAIN!
NO! I'LL GO BROKE!
BRIEFS
THANK YOU, KAKIE! TRULY, YOU ARE A CREDIT TO MONSTERS WHO EAT CAKE EVERYWHERE!
HEY, I WAS ALWAYS ABOUT THE FANS, ANYWAY.

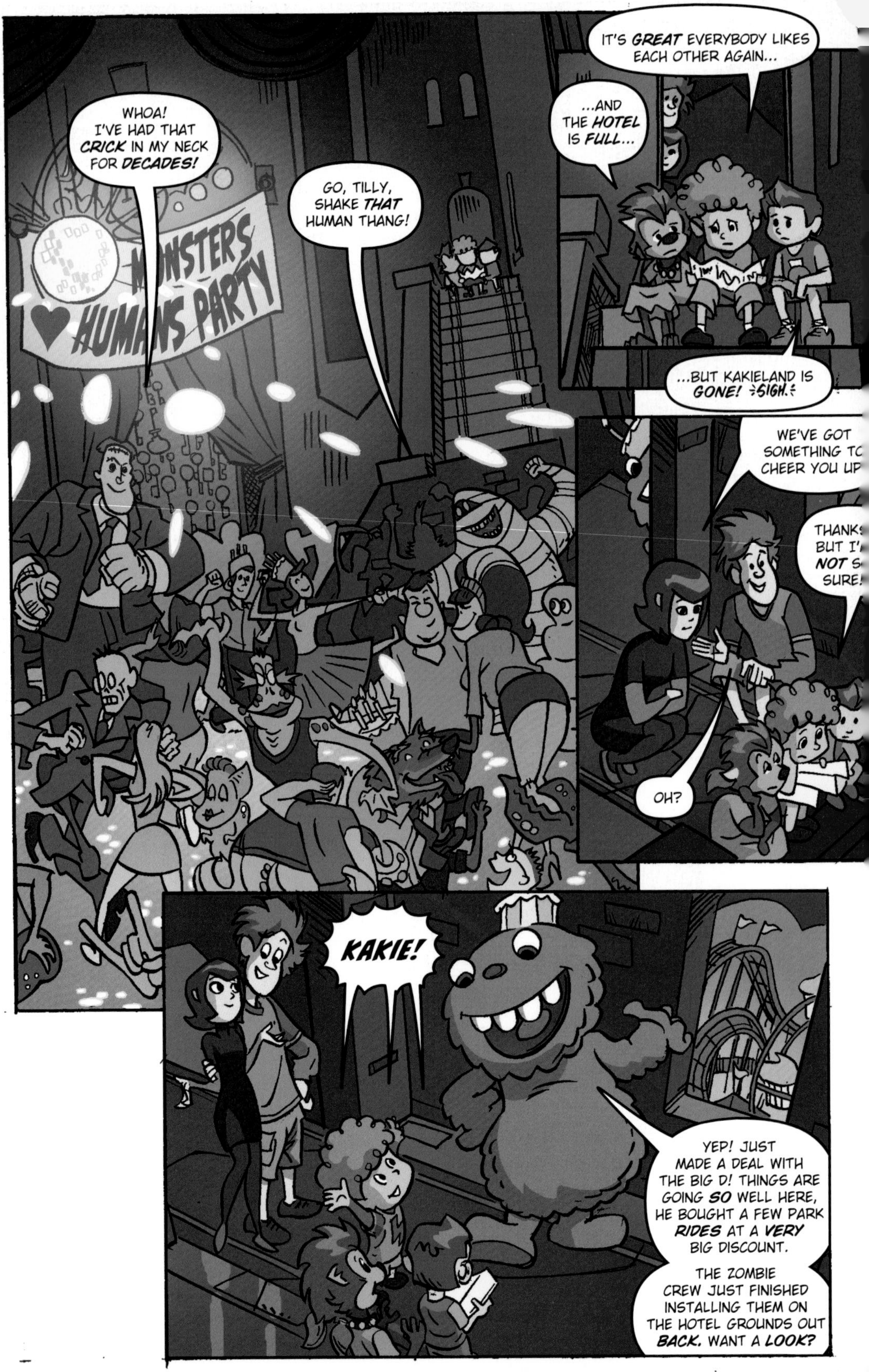
WHOA! I'VE HAD THAT CRICK IN MY NECK FOR DECADES!
MONSTERS ♥ HUMANS PARTY
GO, TILLY, SHAKE THAT HUMAN THANG!
IT'S GREAT EVERYBODY LIKES EACH OTHER AGAIN...
...AND THE HOTEL IS FULL...
...BUT KAKIELAND IS GONE! SIGH.
WE'VE GOT SOMETHING TO CHEER YOU UP
THANKS BUT I'M NOT SO SURE!
OH?
KAKIE!
YEP! JUST MADE A DEAL WITH THE BIG D! THINGS ARE GOING SO WELL HERE, HE BOUGHT A FEW PARK RIDES AT A VERY BIG DISCOUNT.
THE ZOMBIE CREW JUST FINISHED INSTALLING THEM ON THE HOTEL GROUNDS OUT BACK. WANT A LOOK?

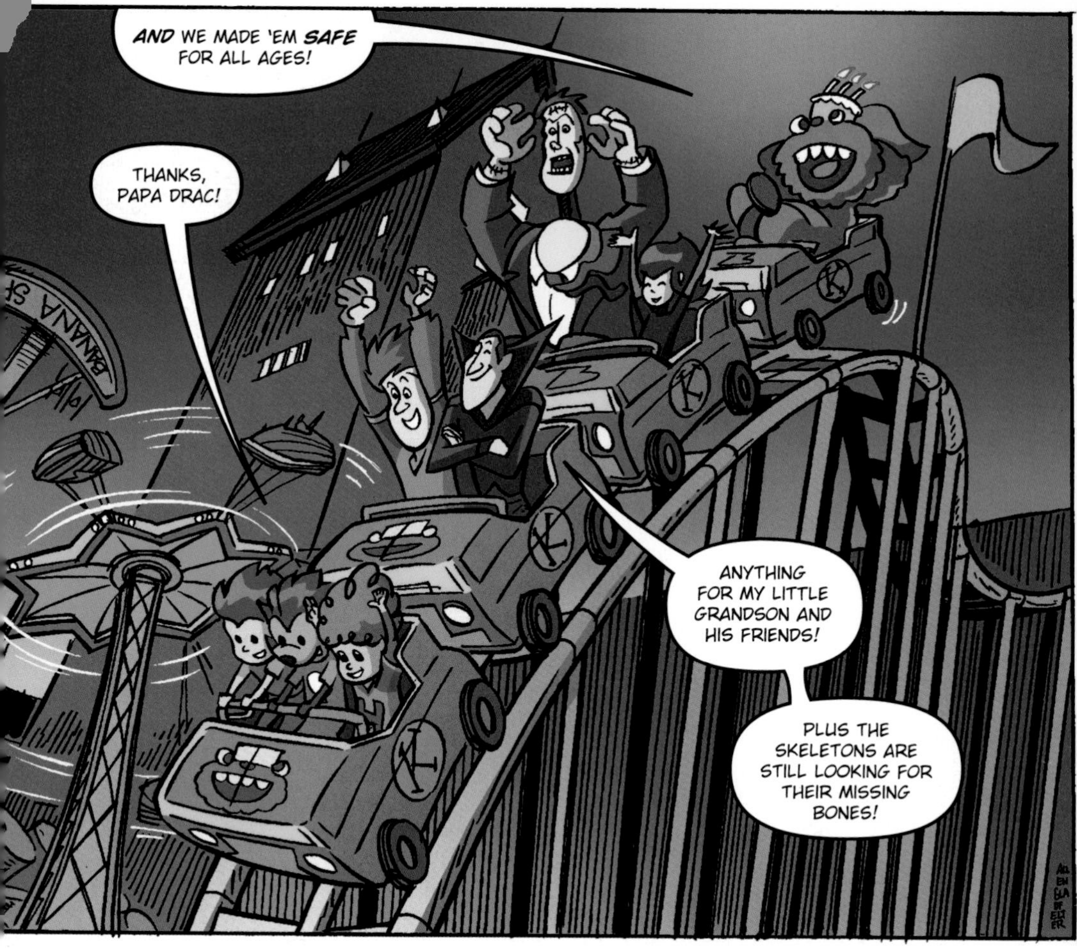
AND WE MADE 'EM SAFE FOR ALL AGES!
THANKS, PAPA DRAC!
ANYTHING FOR MY LITTLE GRANDSON AND HIS FRIENDS!
PLUS THE SKELETONS ARE STILL LOOKING FOR THEIR MISSING BONES!

MEANWHILE, IN THE MARZIPAN MIRROR MAZE...

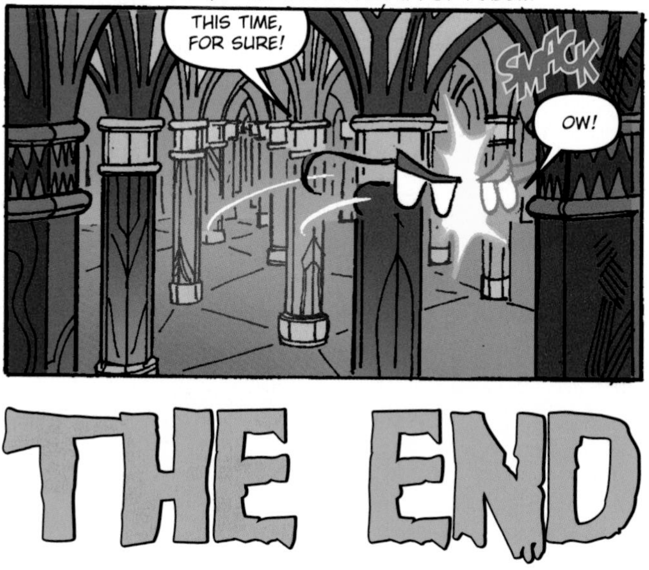
THIS TIME, FOR SURE!
SMACK
OW!

THE END

WATCH OUT FOR PAPERCUTZ

Welcome to HOTEL TRANSYLVANIA, or more accurately, welcome to the premiere HOTEL TRANSYLVANIA graphic novel, by Stefan Petrucha, writer, and Allen Gladfelter, artist, from Papercutz—those monstrously-talented madmen and women dedicated to publishing graphic novels for all ages. I'm Jim Salicrup, Editor-in-Chief and part-time room service employee at the HOTEL TRANSYLVANIA. I'm here to share a personal behind-the-scenes story, recommend a few monstrous Papercutz graphic novels, and offer up some HOTEL TRANSYLVANIA news, in that order…

Longtime Papercutz fans may know that writer Stefan Petrucha and I were childhood friends. I have many great memories of us making comics together when we were kids, but we were also fans of monsters. We loved all sorts of monster stories, monster movies, monster TV shows, and, of course, monster comicbooks. Stefan, I think, loved monsters even more than I did. While after school I would often watch *The Mike Douglas Show*, a talk show that would feature guests such as Moe Howard of the Three Stooges and John Lennon of the Beatles, Stefan was a faithful fan of *Dark Shadows*, a soap opera that featured vampires and werewolves. Together, we've seen many a Frankenstein movie over the years, and Stefan even wrote the novel *"The Shadow of Frankenstein,"* an official sequel to the classic Frankenstein film starring Boris Karloff, so when it came time to choose the perfect comics writer for the HOTEL TRANSYLVANIA, I didn't have to think twice—Stefan is my go-to Monster-Writer! To learn more about Stefan, check out his website at www.petrucha.com.

At Papercutz, we've enjoyed publishing all sorts of graphic novels featuring monsters. We published a series of CLASSICS ILLUSTRATED graphic novels—one series featured 48-page adaptations, and the other featured far-longer comics adaptations of these classic novels: In CLASSICS ILLUSTRATED #2, we featured H.G. Wells's "The Invisible Man," adapted by Rick Geary; in #4, Edgar Allan Poe's "The Raven and Other Poems," illustrated by Gahan Wilson; in #7, Robert Louis Stevenson's "Dr. Jekyll & Mr. Hyde," adapted by John K. Snyder III; and in #12, H.G. Wells's "The Island of Dr. Moreau," adapted by Steven Grant and Eric Vincent. In CLASSICS ILLUSTRATED DELUXE #3, Mary Shelley's "Frankenstein," adapted by Marion Mousse; and in #10, Edgar Allan Poe's "The Murders in the Rue Morgue and Other Tales," adapted by Morvan & Druet, and Corbeyran & Marcel. We also published four funny MONSTER graphic novels by brilliant cartoonist Lewis Trondheim, in which a special powder is able to bring any drawing, especially those of monsters, to life. Many of these great graphic novels may now be out-of-print, but worth finding at your local library.

Easier to find are the more recent Papercutz graphic novels such as the two volumes of THE LUNCH WITCH by Deb Lucke, about an out-of-work witch who decides to make ends meet by becoming a school lunch lady. And there's DRACULA MARRIES FRANKENSTEIN, the latest *Anne of Green Bagels* graphic novel by Susan Schade and John Buller, about Anne and her friend Otto spending their summer making a funny monster movie.

Which brings us back to the HOTEL TRANSYLVANIA movies… These movies have been so popular that HOTEL TRANSYLVANIA 3 is being released in July 2018. But the HOTEL TRANSYLVANIA story doesn't end there (or here)! Now airing on the Disney Channel is an all-new animated TV series inspired by the HOTEL TRANSYLVANIA movies, and Papercutz is proud to announce that we'll be creating all-new graphic novels, by Stefan Petrucha and Allen Gladfelter, inspired by the TV series! So, if you love Drac, Mavis, Frank, Murray, Wayne, and all the rest, as much as we do, this is the greatest news of all! The TV series is actually expanding the HOTEL TRANSYLVANIA universe in a way we're sure you're going to enjoy, and we can't wait for you to experience it! So until the next HOTEL TRANSYLVANIA graphic novel (coming soon!), this is your Papercutz Editor-in-Chief saying "Bleh, bleh, bleh!"

Thanks,

Jim

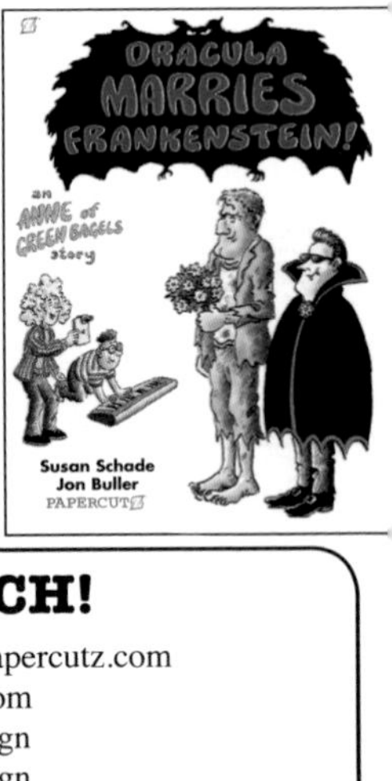
DRACULA MARRIES FRANKENSTEIN!
an ANNE of GREEN BAGELS story
Susan Schade
Jon Buller
PAPERCUTZ

STAY IN TOUCH!

EMAIL: salicrup@papercutz.com
WEB: papercutz.com
INSTAGRAM: @papercutzgn
TWITTER: @papercutzgn
FACEBOOK: PAPERCUTZGRAPHICNOVELS
FAN MAIL: Papercutz, 160 Broadway, Suite 700, East Wing, New York, NY 10038